D1216514

Murder by the Dozen

© 2013
Cover Image © Bryce Pearson

Black Curtain Press
P.O. Box 632
Floyd, VA 24091

ISBN 13: 978-1627555470

First Edition
10 9 8 7 6 5 4 3 2 1

Murder by the Dozen

Hugh Wiley

LONG CHANCE	7
TEN BELLS	18
A RAY OF LIGHT	32
THE BELL FROM CHINA	44
THE FEAST OF KALI	57
JAYBIRD'S CHANCE	69
NO WITNESSES	82
THREE WORDS	94
SCORNED WOMAN	107
SEVEN OF SPADES	121
THE THIRTY THOUSAND DOLLAR BOMB	138
MEDIUM WELL DONE	151

LONG CHANCE

Trouble with a thrust bearing held the Palomita in the open sea seventy miles out of San Francisco Bay for three sunlit days and three clear nights. On the fourth evening of her distress, Monday night, a dripping fog obscured the crescent moon. The fog seemed to have a curative effect on the Palomita's thrust bearings. Before midnight, under a slow bell, she nosed through the Golden Gate.

Barely under steerage way a sudden activity replaced the quiet on the ship's forward deck. A power launch drifted out of the night and nestled against the Palomita's quarter. The launch, trailing on a line, slid aft along the tramp's rusty hull for eighty feet and then held her position for eighteen minutes. When the launch cast off and stood away from the steamer she carried a hundred Chinese who had come over the ship's side. Within the hour these men had become members of the Chinese colony in San Francisco.

The enterprise should have been accomplished with complete secrecy, but before the launch had landed its Chinese cargo the wireless operator on the Palomita had tied in with a short-wave set in a Japanese residence on Fillmore Street. Forty words in private code went through with only casual interference at that hour, to the alert ears of Amano Kimura. To the world at large Mr. Kimura was a recognized authority on various branches of oriental art.

Immediately upon receipt of the message from the wireless operator of the Palomita, Mr. Kimura's interest in oriental art gave place to a sudden activity in connection with a more material project. Forthwith he left his apartment in the Fillmore Street house and headed for Chinatown.

On Tuesday morning at nine o'clock in his San Francisco apartment James Lee Wong received Sam Wing. Facing his diminutive Chinese countryman, James Lee smiled. “The years have been kind to you,” he said. “You look younger than you did in your freshman year.”

“Yale was a grind,” Sam Wing answered. “Too much night work.”

“And now each night as chief of aviation for the Nanking Government you enjoy eight or ten hours of sound, refreshing sleep?” Irony tempered the speaker's smile. “I hope that you will not sleep too much.”

Sam Wing scowled. “I have slept too much,” he admitted. “I need your help. Can I tell you my story—off the record?”

After a moment, “On the pay roll of the United States Government I am an operative in the Department of Justice,” James Lee answered. “In this room for the moment I am your former classmate and your friend. Tell your story.”

“Do you know Edgar Parmill?”

“I met him in Shanghai six years ago. One of the greatest flyers in the world. Is he in town?”

“Parmill and I came in from China last week,” Sam Wing said.

“He works for you?”

“He works with me. Nominally I'm his chief. Actually he knows more aviation in ten minutes than I'll learn in a lifetime. We came over to buy four bombing planes from the Meteor people. Parmill has been under cover at the Palace Hotel since he got here. I have been here on Grant Avenue. One of the Meteor representatives is down from Seattle.”

“Where is he?”

“At the Palace. We were to have signed the contract for the four planes this morning. Parmill didn't show up.”

James Lee nodded. “And Parmill has the money. It's a cash transaction, I suppose. What is the price of the four planes?”

“Twenty-five thousand apiece. Parmill had a hundred thousand in cash at one o'clock this morning—but please do not suggest...”

“You never can tell....”

“You can tell with Parmill,” Sam Wing declared vehemently. “A million in gold would not buy that man. It's been tried.”

“Parmill does not happen to be a Chinese patriot by any chance, does he?”

Sam Wing frowned. Facing his tall companion, "You never believed in anything," he accused. "You were always that way. You never gave any man credit for decent motives. Parmill is one of China's greatest friends. He is my friend."

"A hundred thousand dollars, is a lot of money." James Lee yawned and reached for a cigarette. "Speaking of my beliefs—I believe in human nature," he suggested.

Sam Wing paced the length of the room. Returning, he looked straight at James Lee. "I think I made a mistake coming to you," he said.

James Lee nodded. "You've made several mistakes in your time. Your stupidity is notorious in Tokyo. Your mistake of last night is a perfect example of your stupidity."

"What do you mean?"

"That gold-bearing cargo of Cantonese that came ashore from the Palomita."

"You know about that?"

"There is a report of it on my desk over there."

A look of fear clouded Sam Wing's eyes. "Jim," he said, "you wouldn't..."

James Lee shook his head. "No, I wouldn't," he said reassuringly. "Maybe you forget that you're in the house of a friend."

"Then for the sake of friendship find Parmill for me. Our people care nothing about the money. Find Parmill for us. We need him."

"Where did you see him last?"

"There was a midnight banquet—half a dozen of the Five Family men, three or four of the Friends of China crew, an American man, old Sing Lung, Parmill and I."

"Where was this?"

"In the Five Family banquet hall in the house of Sing Lung."

"Who was the American?"

"Egan Rylett. He gave ten thousand dollars to the Cause last year."

James Lee nodded. "That was last year," he suggested. "What happened?"

"Specifically, somewhere around one o'clock old Sing Lung and some more of the Five Family men opened the Tong safe and handed over a hundred thousand dollars."

"Handed it to Parmill?"

Sam Wing nodded. "Yes. Parmill and I counted it. He put the money in his pocket. He left Sing Lung's place ten or fifteen minutes later in a taxicab. We were to have breakfast together this morning at eight o'clock. Our date with the Meteor man was for nine o'clock. I telephoned Parmill's room at eight o'clock and there was no answer. One of the hotel men opened the room for me at eight-thirty. Parmill had not slept in his bed. I don't think he returned to the hotel. If he did no one saw him."

James Lee was silent for a moment and then, "Sounds like a tough one," he said. "Let's go over and have a talk with Sing Lung."

Sam Wing's eyes lighted. "You will help me?"

James Lee nodded. "I'll do what I can," he promised.

Sing Lung, nominal head of the Five Family clan, greeted James Lee and Sam Wing in the reception-room of his house. Phrases spoken according to the ritual of Right Conduct used up the first two minutes of the meeting and then, replacing his steel-bowed spectacles, "How may I serve you?" Sing Lung asked.

"Edgar Parmill, the American, has disappeared," James Lee said.

Sing Lung's eyes widened. "With the money?"

"With the money—but that is of no consequence compared to his safety," Sam Wing interposed. "Mr. Lee would like to talk to the taxi driver who took Mr. Parmill to the Palace Hotel. Can you find him?"

Old Sing Lung nodded. "Easily enough. He sleeps every morning in a room rented from my cousin. He will be here in ten minutes."

Addressing the taxi driver, a free-lancing pirate of Grant Avenue's night life, ten minutes later, "You are an Italian?" James Lee asked.

"A Serbian."

"Where did you take the American gentleman who left the dinner party last night at one o'clock or one-fifteen'"

"He wanted to go to the Palace Hotel. He said the Montgomery Street entrance."

“Did you take him to the Palace?”

“He stopped me half a block before we got to Market Street. He said he wanted to get some cigarettes.”

“Did you get them for him?”

“He got out and paid me off. He said he would get his cigarettes and walk across Market Street to the Palace.”

“Did you see what shop he went to?”

“I never seen him after he paid me. I turned around and beat it back, to my stand.”

James Lee nodded at the man. “That's all,” he said.

When the Serbian had left, “Somebody got Parmill between the cigar store and the hotel,” Sam Wing suggested.

James Lee nodded. “Probably. That doesn't help us much.”

“What about talking to the cops on that beat?”

“Not yet,” Lee answered. “I think I'd like to see Mr. Rylett. Call him up and make a date for me, will you?”

“You going to tell him that Parmill has disappeared?”

“He probably knows it.”

“I don't think so.”

“How long has he known Parmill?”

“He never met him before last night. Rylett doesn't like many people. He's rich enough so that he doesn't have to. Parmill made a hit with him. They talked Chinese art and stone-age stuff for an hour together. Rylett is a nut on Chinese archeology. When he found out that Parmill had opened up a string of graves in Kansu he went deaf to everything else.”

“Rig up a date for me,” James Lee repeated. “I may introduce a dash of art into my conversation with Mr. Rylett.” Smiling grimly, “Stone-age stuff.”

“You sound like Rylett was a member of the enemy camp,” Sam Wing objected. “He is a friend of China.”

James Lee scowled. “China has various sorts of friends.”

“You're still capable of a little twisted thinking.”

James Lee's eyes narrowed. “No doubt,” he admitted. “Get on the phone and see what you can do with Rylett. Date me for dinner if you can.”

Greeting Mr. Lee at eight o'clock that evening, “I am delighted to have you as my guest,” Egan Rylett said. “Most opportune! Mr. Wing tells me you are interested in Chinese art. Happy coincidence! Amano Kimura is dining with us tonight. You've heard of him—the great Japanese authority on Han pottery and the earlier Chinese bronzes.

"Everyone has heard of him," James Lee complimented. "I thought he was still in Peru." Clawing through the archives of his memory for another Kimura item, "The monograph on Peruvian pottery—Kimura did some work in that field years ago, if I remember."

Egan Rylett beamed with pleasure and with a quick vicarious pride in this tribute to Amano Kimura. "Two men today—two men alone are masters on that subject! Kimura is one of them."

Meeting Amano Kimura, James Lee shook hands with the Japanese. "I am honored," he said. "How is your work in Peru?"

"Very happy to meet the distinguished Mr. James Lee," Kimura declared. "I have had some success in Peru." He lifted a cigarette to his lips and devoted the next four seconds to an obvious enjoyment of its aroma.

A thin drift of smoke from Kimura's cigarette wavered toward James Lee. "Interesting cigarette," the Chinese reflected. "Indian grown—with a dash of majoon. Gunjah." To Kimura, quickly, and without being conscious of the impulse that prompted the question, "You have lived in Calcutta?"

Kimura looked up at James Lee. A faint expression of surprise marked his reply.

"For a year. Why?"

Regretting his ill-timed inquiry, James Lee resorted to a lie: "A friend of mine in Calcutta, Semple Wainwright, told me about your researches in Peru."

"Mr. Kimura has lived in Peru for five years," Egan Rylett interposed.

At this, glancing at Rylett and then looking up at James Lee through narrowed eyelids, "Your friend Wainwright is also a secret operative for the Department of Justice? Or should I say 'secret'?"

Before James Lee could reply, Egan Rylett stepped away from his two guests. He looked at James Lee in undisguised surprise. "You are an agent of the Department, Mr. Lee?"

The Chinese nodded at his host. “Everyone seems to know that.”

“But Sam Wing said that you were an authority on...”

“I must confess that I am only an amateur in Chinese art. It is, let us say, my pleasure—not my vocation.”

The moment became frozen. Lee damned himself for the maladroit inquiry that had been prompted by the scent of Amano Kimura's cigarette. Then leaping into the silence with a patent air of frankness, “The Department has several of us out here covering the San Francisco-Denver gold transfer,” he explained. “Carrying millions of dollars in gold hundreds of miles is a tempting opportunity for some of the country's bad actors.”

“Two billion dollars in gold, isn't it?” Egan Rylett did the best he could to thaw the frozen moment. “May I offer you cocktails before we dine?”

The cocktails were served in chilled cups of white jade.

“These are delicious,” James Lee complimented. “I have never tasted such an intriguing combination of flavors. Am I wrong in congratulating you on a successful combination of bourbon and Curacao?”

Egan Rylett smiled. “The chocolate flavor betrays it,” he suggested.

“Chocolate? Cinnamon, mace, cloves, perhaps—but no chocolate.”

“There must be chocolate in it,” Rylett insisted. “Let me get a book I have. Strange that neither one of us seems to know what is in curacao.... No matter. May I offer you a second one?”

James Lee bowed. “Thank you.”

“Will you look it up in the encyclopedia, Mr. Lee? I'll be back in a moment. I want to see if my butler knows anything about this stuff. You'll find the encyclopedia over by that window.”

On page 62 of volume 6 of the encyclopedia under “Curacao” James Lee read three lines of the text aloud to Amano Kimura: “A well-known and palatable liqueur, made from orange peel by digesting it in sweetened spirits, with certain spices...” and here his reading was interrupted by a quick sneeze.

"That cigarette of Kimura's is very pungent," the Chinese reflected, realizing that a strong scent of hashish had made him sneeze.

"... as cinnamon, mace, or cloves," he continued. He looked up quickly, "Forgive me," he apologized. His eyes fell again to the text in the open book. An inch under "Curacao" he read "Curare, a celebrated poison used by some tribes of South America '... causing complete paralysis without affecting consciousness...."

Returning from his interview with his butler, "You're right, Mr. Lee," Egan Rylett admitted. "There is no chocolate in curacao. Here I am sixty years old-a man with a fair knowledge of such things and up to this moment I have believed that curacao contained chocolate."

"According to the encyclopedia it contains an essence of orange peel and cinnamon and other spices. Chocolate isn't mentioned. Perhaps you confuse curacao with cacao."

"Perhaps that is it.... Dinner is announced. Shall we go in?"

As the dinner progressed, Lee became increasingly conscious of the problem that faced him. Under the small talk, of which there was a minimum, and the heavier conversation, his thoughts reverted incessantly to the fate of Edgar Parmill. "*Where is Parmill? If these men got Parmill, how did they get him*?"

In the interval preceding dessert Lee contemplated subjecting Egan Rylett to a brief interrogation relative to his association with Edgar Parmill and the purchase of the bombing planes. After a moment's thought he doubted the advisability of mentioning Parmill's name. He thought of the twin machine guns mentioned in the specifications. He remembered a phrase that Sam Wing had used—"synchronized to fire through the propeller arc." He realized that he must time any inquiry relative to Parmill with a similar precision. "Or why not release a hundred-pound demolition bomb and be done with it?" Instinct told him that he was nearing the battle ground. "*Who is Kimura? What a fool I am! He's a shark on archeology—but what else is he*?"

Egan Rylett's butler spoke quietly to his master. Turning to James Lee, "There is a telephone call for you, Mr. Lee," Rylett said. Then, "Sam Wing is calling you. May I have the telephone brought here to the table?"

"That was a bit crude," the Chinese reflected. Aloud, "Thank you, yes."

Over the telephone, "The police have found Parmill," Sam Wing said. "Are you alone?"

"Two loads on the bomb rack mounted right and left," Lee answered. "That clause was in the specifications."

"I understand. Parmill is in the Emergency Hospital. He has been drugged with something that left him paralyzed. He is still alive and conscious. The Chronicle and the Examiner had extras on the street ten minutes ago. The police know who Parmill is. I believe they are turning the case over to the State Department."

Instantly, taking a long chance, inspired by an unaccountable impulse, "You will find the address of the Portuguese agents in Potter's Directory," James Lee said. "Caroval was the high man when I knew the outfit. Vao Caroval. V-a-o C-a-r-o-v-a-1."

"I get you."

"I will return to my apartment around midnight. If I can be of any further help let me know.... I have my own car. See you later."

Returning the telephone to Rylett's butler, who stood beside his chair, "Sam Wing is a bargain hunter," Lee announced. "He is on the trail of a dozen secondhand planes that are owned by a Portuguese outfit," Lee explained. "Sorry to interrupt. Incidentally, do either of you happen to know Vao Caroval?"

"I do not know him," Rylett said.

"A Portuguese gentleman, you say?" Something in Kimura's question sent an honest thrill of fear down James Lee's spine.

"I think he is a Portuguese—of some Latin stock at any rate."

"Vao and Caroval are native names for a South American poison known as curare in the Materia Medica," Kimura explained, smiling in a superior manner. "The Potter who publishes the directory you mentioned would not be related to the distinguished author of the book on poisons and various medical works?"

At this question a burden of doubt seemed to lift from James Lee's heart. He realized instantly that his problem was simplified. He sought quickly to follow his advantage with the impelling force of a direct question. Facing Kimura, "Why did you kill Edgar Parmill?" he asked.

From his left, "Mr. Lee! What do you mean?" Egan Rylett demanded. "Do you insinuate..."

The rest of Rylett's question was drowned in a series of explosions that boomed from the muzzle of a .30-caliber automatic in Amano Kimura's hand. The Japanese held the gun steady on the edge of the table. The gun was aimed at James Lee's heart. Kimura fired five shots before the grimace of hatred in his face changed to a sardonic smile of physical anguish when his fire was returned from a weapon in his opponent's hand.

James Lee put his heavy service .45 back into its holster slung under his left armpit. He turned to Egan Rylett. "If you will be kind enough to pour a glass of brandy for Kimura perhaps we can keep him alive for a while. I would like to force a confession out of him—to keep the records straight."

Rylett, his eyes wide with terror, was backing slowly away from James Lee. "Keep him alive?" he questioned thickly. And then, "But you—aren't you shot?"

"Steel vest," Lee said briefly. "Dented a little bit perhaps, but that's all.... Mr. Rylett, I must apologize for this messy affair—but Edgar Parmill is dying. Kimura got him. Poisoned him with curare."

An hour after midnight, in his apartment on Grant Avenue, facing Sam Wing, "Rylett had nothing to do with Parmill's murder," James Lee declared. "Kimura's confession clears him."

"Where is the hundred thousand?"

"Kimura had it in his pocket. Here it is—with my compliments."

"China thanks you. This means four bombing planes for use against her enemies."

"You'd better cut out the midnight immigration stuff or I'll have to look you over officially. Why not use more of Rylett's money?"

Sam Wing smiled. "If it will clear your conscience, we're shipping a hundred of our countrymen, fighters, back to China on the Tenyo Maru.... My God, Jimmy, you were playing against heavy odds."

"Not so heavy. My own ignorance was the main obstacle. I should have known about Kimura's tie-up with Tokyo. As it happens, I'm lucky—Kimura dug his own grave. Curare. The fool made his big mistake in his question about Major Potter—you remember when I mentioned Vao Caroval over the telephone? Ego. Kimura had to show me then and there that he knew more about South American arrow poisons than I did. Vao and Caroval—curare has fifty names.... Poor Parmill."

"Terrible," Sam Wing commented. "Lying there completely conscious, wide awake, utterly helpless—paralyzed."

"Kimura confessed that he got him with a jab in the shoulder two minutes after Parmill got out of that taxicab."

"I'm sorry you didn't torture that Jap for a while."

"The blow-off wasn't easy for him. I promised him I'd see that his chief in the Javanese Foreign Office got a copy of his confession. That was torture enough for the egotistical little rat!"

"I'm glad of that," Sam Wing declared. Then, after a moment, "You surely took a long chance. The odds were a million to one against you."

James Lee smiled. "Kimura dug his own grave—after the trifling little curacao argument.... You remember that night in New Haven when I drew the jack of diamonds in a stud game and made a straight flush? Those things happen now and then. Just plain lucky."

"You make me sick! What do you think I am, a sucker? Just slip me that ring and I'll be on my way. We're through!"

"But, Tommy darling, I've told you that ..."

"Don't Tommy darling me! Three nights at the Coconut Grove with the louse. Five or six times at Zenger's beach house—and God knows where else. Three, four, five o'clock in the morning and nobody answers but your mother when I call you up. Party girl! Give me back that ring! I'm through! Our engagement's busted. Give me back that ring before Mercer nicks it. The perfumed frog! If I wasn't all through with you I'd blast his heart out!"

Tommy Hale grabbed the girl's left wrist and tore a half-carat diamond ring off her finger. "There! From now on enjoy yourself with Mercer and anybody that is fool enough to string along with you!"

There were tears in Sally Chapman's eyes as she began bravely enough a recital of the truth. "I went out with Pierre Mercer because he said there was a good part for me in a picture. Zenger is directing it. He told Mercer to coach me for the voice tests. We could get married on the..."

"Voice tests with a full orchestra! Voice tests in Coconut Grove—and where else? Big shot in the bedroom scenes! You make me sick! I'd give Mercer a voice test with a .38 bullet through his throat if you were worth it! You rotten little liar! Us get married on your salary contract!" Tommy Hale's mouth curled in scorn. "All-night party girl!... So long!"

Tommy Hale stumbled down the steps that led to the street level from Sally Chapman's second-story apartment. He proceeded to add six slugs of bourbon to the preliminary six that he had carried into the battle with him.

At nine o'clock next morning he carried the biggest hangover that had ever been seep in the Galaxy Productions studio. Scene Thirteen of Death for Love was all set for action.

Tommy Hale, functioning as property man, was all set for trouble.

A night of nerves and tears had been Sally Chapman's dividend of anguish. “Tommy will come back to you,” her mother had comforted.

“He thinks I lied to him about Mercer,” the girl sobbed. “Now it's all finished.”

All finished except the sequel which began in Scene Thirteen of Death for Love.

In Death for Love a lady's honor was involved, as usual. Vernon Zenger, directing the picture for Galaxy Productions, had hit upon the novel expedient of pistols for two as a means whereby the sullied name of the heroine might be restored to its pristine purity.

Walter Lodge, a visiting American running wild in Paris, had been challenged by Pierre Mercer. The duel scene had been rehearsed half a dozen times. With each rehearsal it became more evident that Death for Love was a comedy instead of a gripping drama of human hearts. With each discharge, of the duelists' pistols, Vernon Zenger, the director, seemed to realize that his reputation was being riddled with bullets.

At eleven o'clock, after indulging in a loud and bitter criticism of the manner, in which Walter Lodge, the visiting American, played his part, the director brushed this half of the dueling duet into a ringside seat. “I'll show you how I want it done,” Zenger barked. “Give me that gun!” He grabbed the long-barreled single-shot .38 pistol from Lodge's hand.

Zenger walked over toward Tommy Hale, the property man. “Load this gun,” he ordered. He beckoned to Pierre Mercer. “Bring that other pistol over here and let Tommy load it with another blank.”

When the two pistols were loaded, reciting part of Rule Eighteen of the Code Duello as adopted at Clonmel in 1777, “Firing may be regulated first by signal, second by word of command,” Zenger admonished, addressing Pierre Mercer and his side-tracked opponent. “The word of command is 'Fire!' It is not necessary to pull the trigger of your pistol at that instant. Take deliberate aim before you shoot.... Ready? Let's go. Back to back, Mercer. March away five paces and, as you face about, the seconds together will give the command to fire. Come out here—keep your right arm pointing straight down.... Back to back... five paces now. Let's go!"

Marching apart, Zenger with a stride reminiscent of the Prussian goose-step, Mercer in the easy route step of the French army, the duelists halted at the fifth pace and wheeled to face each other. "Watch this, Walter!" the director cautioned. "Take it easy, Mercer. Don't hurry, you've got to get your aim."

Following the seconds' command to fire, Pierre Mercer lifted his pistol above his head and lowered it slowly, until it pointed finally at Vernon Zenger's heart. Approximating this action, but going through it more slowly than his opponent, Vernon Zenger's weapon lined up on Mercer's heart three seconds after the Frenchman had fired. "Deliberately, like this," Zenger admonished for Walter Lodge's benefit. "There is no hurry. Your aim must be true." With this, sighting his pistol straight at Pierre Mercer's heart, the director pulled the trigger.

Mercer's pose spoke of contempt for his adversary. His lips were curled in an expression of this contempt. In the script, following his opponent's fire, a bloodstain was to show on Mercer's left shoulder. In this rehearsal, following the bang of the director's pistol, the bloodstain showed over Mercer's heart. The expression, of contempt on his face changed instantly to surprise, and then he fell, crumpled in a heap.

"That's realism," somebody on the side lines exclaimed, admiringly.

A moment later, lifting Pierre Mercer's head, listening in vain for the sound of his beating heart, Walter Lodge, who had been first to gain the side of the fallen man, looked up at the ring of startled faces.

"He's dead!" Lodge announced, horrified. "That gun was loaded! Tommy must have slipped a loaded cartridge into it by mistake!"

Still holding the pistol that had brought death to Mercer, Vernon Zenger looked down at the dead man. His gaze traveled from the dead man's face to the pistol in his hand. He dropped the pistol then and lifted his trembling hand toward Tommy Hale.

"You put a loaded cartridge into that gun!" he accused.

The property man's eyes widened with astonishment. Before surprise had changed to terror, "What do you mean, loaded cartridge? There's nothing but blanks in this box," he protested. "How do you figure I could..."

Interrupting Tommy Hale, Walter Lodge, coolest of the group, waved a stop-signal at the property man. "Shut up!" he ordered. "This is going to be tough for you. You'd better not talk any more than you have to."

Wildly then, rising from beside the dead man, Vernon Zenger continued the attack on Tommy Hale. Following a barrage of profanity, "You've killed him!" Zenger yelled. "You've slaughtered him! You damned, crazy, careless murderer!... Somebody get a doctor. Somebody call the police. Don't stand there! Somebody lend me a hand. Carry him over to that couch. Straighten him out. For the love of God, somebody bring me a drink of whisky. I've got to get a drink. Don't let anybody leave till the police get here. I've got to get a drink!"

Zenger walked off the set. Outside of the studio he turned to his left toward the building that housed the general offices of Galaxy Productions.

In the San Francisco headquarters of the Hazard Guaranty Corporation James Lee Wong faced Ross Mason. The Chinese man, listed more simply on the federal pay rolls as James Lee, smiled at the vice president of the insurance company in thin but friendly sympathy. "I'm afraid you're stuck for the drinks," he said to the white man. "Outside of the owner's liability clause, the government's case is clear. The master of the ship is innocent enough. The opium and the Chinese men were smuggled in by the second officer and two of the engine-room gang. My report puts Captain Parrish in the clear."

"Your report won't clear him with the owners," Ross Mason growled. "He should have watched his crew more carefully. This will cost him his command.... How much will it cost us?"

"Thirty of my Chinese countrymen at a thousand dollars a head," James Lee answered. "The Treasury Department will probably slap a ten-thousand-dollar libel on the ship on account of the opium. It will probably cost you close to forty thousand dollars altogether, less your insurance premium."

Ross Mason groaned. “I'd like to pull the company out of marine risks altogether. Too much of a gamble. Look what the longshoremen in the Pacific ports have done to us.”

“I'm looking at that next week,” James Lee announced. “I'll have to ask you to hold what I tell you about this strike situation in strict confidence. There are some interesting angles to it.”

Mason nodded. “I'll keep my mouth shut. There's some mighty expensive angles to it for us. What are you doing?”

“The Department seems to think that it would be a good idea to round up some of the big-league Communists who are out here on the Coast,” James Lee confided. “I have orders to give the layout a look-see. Los Angeles is the quietest city on the Coast, consequently I have decided to begin my investigation down there.”

At this, brightening for a moment, Ross Mason smiled at James Lee. “I suppose Washington hasn't rigged you up with a shorter work week by any chance?”

The government man shook his head. “I work four or five regular weeks every seven days—when I work.

“Still the human dynamo,” Mason complimented. “Away back in the early days when I first knew you at Yale, none of us ever understood how you seemed to live without sleep.”

“Good days—simple days,” James Lee mused. “That was a long time ago, before life became so complicated.”

“They were grand days,” Ross Mason agreed. After a reminiscent moment of silence, “The Company just picked up another expensive luxury in Los Angeles last week,” he announced. “It's costing us two hundred thousand dollars. We wrote a blanket policy on the cast of a picture for a movie outfit. One of the actors was murdered.”

“You refer to Pierre Mercer, the man whom the director of Galaxy Productions shot by accident in rehearsing a duel scene? The affair where the jealous property man slipped the loaded cartridge into the pistol instead of a blank?”

Ross Mason nodded. “It's the Mercer case. Galaxy Productions demands payment for the full amount of the policy—two hundred thousand bucks.”

“That's a lot of money,” James Lee said. “Movie stars seem to be worth more than smuggled Chinese.”

"Jimmy, I wonder if you'd have time to look the Galaxy layout over for me." Ross Mason reached for a cigarette and lighted it.

James Lee's eyes narrowed. "Two hundred thousand dollars," he said. "It seems to me you need a banker more than you need me. Who is back of Galaxy Productions?"

"It's a one-man outfit. Lamon Ward is the man. He's president of Galaxy Productions. It's sort of a shoe-string affair. They made two or three quick ones last fall. Ward is head of the outfit and Vernon Zenger is their one and only director. They release through one of the larger companies. They were about halfway through this Death for Love picture when Mercer was killed. I can't see where they stand to lose two hundred thousand."

"Is that the only angle that interests you?"

Mason looked quickly at James Lee. "What do you mean?"

"Nothing much," James Lee said. "What do you know about Zenger?"

"He's an imported luxury," Mason announced. "Lamon Ward signed him up in Germany last year."

James Lee nodded. "What do you know about Lamon Ward?"

"Quite a lot," the insurance man affirmed. "He owned a shoe store in Chicago ten years ago. It blew up. He started a string of dyeing and cleaning joints and made a lot of money until some of the Chicago boys dynamited three of his places. He made a long jump out of the front line trenches of that war and landed in Hollywood. Up to three years ago he had a string of beauty parlors. He made an assignment for the creditors when beauty began to sell at a loss. Since then he's been fluttering around in the picture game one way and another. He's a two-spot in the Hollywood deck, but it looks like his bad luck with Mercer will cost the Hazard Guaranty Corporation two hundred thousand dollars."

"Sounds like he's an interesting character," James Lee commented. "I'll look him up for my own amusement while I'm in Los Angeles. I'll let you know what I think of him when I get back."

James Lee got up and held out his hand to Ross Mason. "See you next week," he said briefly. Amending this, "See you next week—unless some of the local talent in the Communist crew rig up a vacation for me."

In Los Angeles following a ten-minute confidential conversation with the Collector of United States Internal Revenue, James Lee was equipped with a document that carried him safely through the outer turmoil of Galaxy Productions, straight to the private office of Lamon Ward.

Facing the producer, "I know you are a busy man, Mr. Ward, and I'll try to make our interview as brief as possible," Lee said. "I want to ask you about two or three minor items in your last year's income-tax return. It is possible that you have a refund coming from the government." Smiling at Mr. Ward, "Strangely enough the government makes mistakes now and then."

The picture man shook hands with his visitor. "That sounds like good news," he said. "Will you have a cigar?"

James Lee elected to smoke a cigar. After he had lighted it he dived into a complex dissertation wherein several items in Lamon Ward's individual income-tax return for the previous year became hopelessly tangled with the corporation income-tax return of Galaxy Productions.

Concluding his oration, "We have a recent Treasury ruling that will interest you. It should save you several hundred dollars. That's our bad luck, of course, but we are primarily interested in keeping the records straight."

Lamon Ward smiled pleasantly through a haze of cigar smoke. "That's the first good news I've had since Tiger was a pup," he said to James Lee. "All going out and nothing coming in is the theme song we've been hearing."

James Lee nodded sympathetically. "I know—the picture game is mighty tough on the producer's bank roll. The public doesn't know a thing about what it costs to make a big picture."

"Tough and then some! In this game right when a man thinks he's heading for a rake-off, something happens and before he knows it he skids into the red up to his neck. Look what happened on this picture we're shooting at the present time. Everything lined up for the home stretch and one of the leading characters gets himself killed!"

James Lee's countenance was a mask of interested innocence.

"I suppose there's no such thing as insurance on your actors while you're making a film?"

"Of course there's insurance," Ward returned. "I'll collect two hundred thousand from the Hazard Guaranty outfit on Mercer's accident, but what of it? That still leaves the books a long ways from the black ink."

James Lee's eyes widened in amazement. "I'd no idea pictures cost that much," he said. "It must be a terribly interesting game of heavyweight poker, playing for stakes like that."

"It is a terribly interesting game. Have you ever watched an outfit shoot a picture?"

"I never had the luck to be invited."

"Would you like to see them shooting Death for Love?"

"Nothing I'd like better."

Lamon Ward got to his feet. "Come along. I'll introduce you to Vernon Zenger. He's the director. He's a big shot in the picture game. I discovered him in Germany. I'll introduce you to him and you can see what makes the wheels go round in a picture studio."

A moment after his introduction to the director, James Lee reached into the left pocket of his coat and hauled out a polished silver cigarette case. He handed it to Zenger. "Will you have a cigarette, Mr. Zenger?" he asked.

The director smiled and shook his head. He handed the case back to James Lee. "Thanks," he said. "We don't smoke while the cameras are working."

"Sorry," James Lee said. "Thoughtless of me. Three or four cigarettes with smoke drifting all over the shop and every scene would look like the Chicago fire. I suppose you have to pay as much attention to keeping the air clean as you do to the floor. That's what that boy is doing over there with the oiled mop, isn't it?" James Lee pointed to a Chinese boy who was erasing a trail of footprints from a waxed floor.

"That's it. We've got to watch every detail. If we don't, the public watches them for us—at our expense."

At seven o'clock that night, James Lee rang the bell of the apartment where Sally Chapman lived with her mother.

"I want to talk with you about your friend Tommy Hale," he said to the girl.

"Are you another reporter?"

"I'm making a confidential investigation of this case for the defense," Lee answered. "You don't believe that Tommy is guilty of murdering Pierre Mercer, do you?"

"He's no more guilty than you are."

"Where did the loaded cartridge come from?"

"I'm tired of that question. That's what everybody asks. How do I know?"

"Tommy loaded the pistol, didn't he? Have you talked with him about that detail?"

"You read what he said to the prosecuting attorney. He'd been loading those pistols all during half a dozen rehearsals of the scene."

"Never mind that question. The district attorney dug up a motive for the murder."

"Tommy was jealous. You mean the times I went out with Mercer?"

James Lee nodded. "It appears that he had reason to be jealous. You dined and danced with Pierre Mercer half a dozen times publicly, didn't you?"

"Of course I did. I went out with him because he wanted to help me with a part in the next picture that Zenger is going to make. Zenger told Mercer to teach me how to use my voice."

"Where did you meet Zenger?"

"I met him in the studio. I called there two or three times when Tommy was going to take me out to supper."

"How did you happen to visit Zenger's house?"

"He told Mercer to bring me out to see him. He wanted to talk to me."

"Mercer was shot on Thursday. When you saw Tommy Wednesday night he threatened to kill Mercer, didn't he?"

"Yes—he was drunk."

"Did Tommy own a .38 revolver or a pistol of that caliber?"

The girl nodded. "He had a .38 revolver that he used to take with him when he went into the mountains."

"So that he might easily have had a few loose .38 cartridges lying around his house?"

"I hadn't thought about that at all. He wouldn't be careless with things like that."

"You mean if he did put a cartridge into the pistol that killed Mercer it would have been a deliberate act on his part—and not carelessness?"

The girl's eyes blazed. "What are you trying to do! Didn't you tell me you were trying to save Tommy's life?"

James Lee bowed. "I am trying to save Tommy's life," he said.

There was some difficulty in locating Wong Bok Chung, but after five unsuccessful telephone calls James Lee managed to get a line through to that eminent member of the Wong family.

After appropriate inquiries regarding the health and well-being of his distinguished countryman, and after a cackling series of felicitations had been enjoyed under the Ritual of Right Conduct, still speaking in the common Cantonese dialect, "I desire to obtain the address of one of our countrymen who dwells within your district," James Lee explained. "His name is Chin Hoy." Lapsing into English, "He is employed in the studio of Galaxy Productions. I wish to see him tonight. I am at the Biltmore Hotel."

"He will visit your room before midnight," Wong Bok Chung promised.

"Long life and plenteous years," James Lee concluded.

At eight minutes after eleven o'clock Chin Hoy knocked on the door of James Lee's room in the Biltmore Hotel.

"How may I serve you?" the visitor asked after he had been admitted to the room.

"I am interested in the regrettable tragedy that involved the death of Pierre Mercer," James Lee answered. "You were present when Mercer was shot, were you not?"

With the memory of the scene masking his face with sorrow, "I saw the white man die," Chin Hoy said.

"Did you see Tommy Hale load the pistol that the director, Vernon Zenger, used?"

"I did not observe that."

"At each rehearsal of the duel, after the pistols were fired, what became of the empty cartridges?"

"Mr. Tommy Hale threw them on the floor. In the course of my work I swept them up."

"What did you do with them?"

The frown on Chin Hoy's olive-tinted brow softened. "I have a little daughter," he said. "She is six years old. I saved the empty cartridges and made a necklace of tinkling bells for her to wear."

James Lee reached in his pocket and produced a roll of currency. He snapped a twenty-dollar bill toward Chin Hoy. "Take this money. Get a taxi cab; go home; bring me that necklace of tinkling bells. Tomorrow you can give your daughter another bit of jewelry to replace the one I want. One moment!... Can you remember how many empty cartridges are in the necklace?"

For ten seconds Chin Hoy stared blankly into the obscure caverns of memory and then, "I bought nine bits of white jade to go between the bells," he said. "There are ten empty cartridges in the necklace. They are hung on a silken cord."

"Did you get them all?"

"I got all of them except the two that were fired at the time of the murder. The police officers kept them and the pistols."

In the hour after midnight Chin Hoy returned with the necklace he had made for Lily Chin out of the empty cartridges. "Here it is," he said, handing the tinkling ornament to James Lee. "And here is also sixteen dollars and eighty cents—your change from the twenty-dollar bill."

"Thank you—keep that money. It will buy a silver necklace for your daughter." James Lee carried the string of empty cartridges to a cone of bright light that flooded the top of a writing desk. In this strong light he studied the empty cartridges for five minutes, examining the metallic shells under an eight-diameter Coddington lens. He reached in his pocket for a knife and cut the silk cord that joined the cartridges and the nine bits of white jade. He handed the jade and the fragments of the cord to Chin Hoy. "You may have these," he said. "Return to your home now. You will say nothing to anyone of what you have done tonight, of what you have seen, of what I have said to you."

Chin Hoy bowed to James Lee. “A wise man understands a nod,” he returned. “I hope Kwan Yin may smile upon you.”

James Lee nodded and held out his hand to his countryman. “Good luck,” he said, shaking hands in the western manner. “Good luck and good night.”

After his visitor had left, James Lee turned again to the ten empty cartridges that lay on the table in the bright glare of the reading lamp. He inspected them once more with his magnifying lens, dividing them into two groups. There were five cartridges in each group. He put them into two envelopes and dropped them into the left pocket of his coat. Then he went to bed.

The next morning at nine o'clock, after he had bathed and breakfasted, he went to the police headquarters. In the office of Lieutenant Crowell, who was in charge of the homicide squad, after he had introduced himself, “I would like to see the exhibits in the Mercer case,” he explained.

“Anything you want is yours,” Lieutenant Crowell answered. “I'm mighty glad to meet you, Mr. Lee. How does it happen you're interested in this Mercer killing?”

“I'm checking up for the Hazard Guaranty people. Mercer's death stuck them for two hundred thousand dollars.” James Lee paused. “Do you think there's a chance of getting a confession out of Hale?”

Lieutenant Crowell grunted.

“He'll take his walk to the gas chamber without breaking. He rigged the murder....”

Interrupting Lieutenant Crowell, one of his clerks came in with the exhibits in the Mercer case. “Here's the gun that Tommy Hale shoved the loaded cartridge into,” the lieutenant explained. “Here's the bullet that the surgeons took out of Mercer's heart. Here's another test bullet we fired to match up the rifling of the pistol. Here's the empty cartridge that held the death bullet and...”

“Let me see that cartridge!”

A close observer might have detected an unusual nervous tension in James Lee's manner at this moment.

Lieutenant Crowell handed him the empty cartridge that had held the death bullet. “Union Metallic .38,” he said, and when James Lee produced his magnifying lens, “You'll see that it is flared a little on the open end. The pistol was chambered for a longer cartridge."

James Lee gave thirty seconds to a careful inspection of the death cartridge, and then he put the cartridge and the magnifying lens on the desk in front of Lieutenant Crowell. "Tommy Hale is innocent," he said quietly. From the left pocket of his coat he hauled out the two envelopes containing the ten empty cartridges that had been part of Lily Chin's necklace. He opened these envelopes. "The Chinese sweeper in the studio saved these shells," he explained. "They were fired in rehearsing the duel scene. Take that lens and look at the impressions of the firing pins in the soft copper caps.... Look at these five empty cartridges from the first pistol.... Now look at this other group. They were fired from the second pistol. Observe the little V-shaped mark that the firing pin made. Remember the two short parallel lines made by the firing pin of the first pistol."

"I see the difference," Lieutenant Crowell said. He picked up the empty cartridge that had held the death bullet. Through the magnifying lens he looked at the impression of the firing pin in the soft copper cap in the end of the empty brass shell for ten seconds and then, voicing the conclusion that followed a brief train of reasoning, "There must have been a third pistol!" he exclaimed. "This differs from both of the other types! The firing pin that hit the copper cap in the death cartridge is different from the other two!" Looking straight at James Lee, "That means there must have been a third pistol," he repeated. "Zenger carried the third gun—and nobody saw him make the switch!"

"Right!" James Lee nodded in agreement with this statement. "If I may suggest the next move, Lieutenant, you will arrest Zenger right away."

"Right away and then some!" Lieutenant Crowell exploded. He reached for one of the telephones on his desk.

"Just one second." James Lee laid his hand on the lieutenant's arm. "It might be well to have your men arrest Lamon Ward along with Zenger—but keep them apart."

After a moment's thought Lieutenant Crowell smiled grimly. "You're right," he said. "Ward would be the one to get the insurance money. I'll bring him in along with Zenger.... You've done a mighty slick piece of work, Mr. Lee."

“Lamon Ward and Zenger did the slick piece of work,” James Lee amended.

“Slick enough,” Lieutenant Crowell agreed. “They only missed the firing pin trick—but you happened to ring the bell with the ace of trumps.”

James Lee smiled at the lieutenant's compliment. To himself, “Ten bells!” he reflected. “The ten tinkling bells of Lily Chin's necklace—the death knell for Ward and Zenger.”

A RAY OF LIGHT

At six o'clock in the evening one of James Lee's assistants rang through from Los Angeles with a progress report on a narcotic case involving men and methods important enough to have interested the Department of Justice. At six-fifteen James Lee's chief rang through to San Francisco with some new dope on a couple of big-shot public enemies who were supposed to be heading for San Francisco. Seven minutes after he had finished this conversation with his chief, Mr. Joseph Temple called him on the telephone.

"I should like to see you for half an hour," Mr. Temple said. "Can you have dinner with me at my house? I have a new consignment of emeralds that might interest you."

"The emeralds sound tempting. I'm working tonight. Are you downtown?"

"I'm in my office."

"Why don't you drop in on your way home?"

"I'll be there in fifteen minutes. I am bringing Meade Capron with me. Not socially—he's part of the plot."

"Bring him along."

When he had hung up the telephone James Lee walked from the living room of his apartment to his kitchen. "Light up the library," he said to his houseboy. "Two gentlemen will be here in a few minutes."

"Cocktails?" the servant asked.

Before James Lee could reply his cook added another question to the house boy's interrogation. "Two men stay for dinner?"

James Lee shook his head at the cook. "No," he said, and then to the younger servant, "No cocktails. It's Mr. Joe Temple. He likes our dry sherry. Take in a decanter of it. Old Meade Capron is with him. I don't know what Mr. Capron drinks."

"Olo man Caplon likee whisky," the Chinese cook announced. "Long time I savvy what he likee."

James Lee smiled. "Take some bourbon in for Mr. Capron," he said to the house boy.

Greeting James Lee, "I'm awfully glad to see you," Joseph Temple declared. "I've got a tough problem for you. Capron will tell you all about it. Mr. Lee—Mr. Capron."

To the elderly Mr. Capron, "I believe I told you that Lee and I were classmates at Yale," Joseph Temple explained. "If any man can find a way out of this mess he can."

In the library of James Lee's apartment, "First of all," Joseph Temple began, "I've got a very serious charge to lay against young Warren Bayne. Do you know him?"

"I've met him. I can't say that I know him," James Lee said. "You mean the young man who is to marry Miss Harwood—Louise Harwood?"

"That's the man. Giddy young fool on the social trapeze."

Lee nodded. "Given to making long swings on the social trapeze from Hollywood to Del Monte to Burlingame to San Francisco."

"And all way points where the polo set do their heavy drinking," Temple added.

"What's he done?"

"He's done a lot of things in the past," Meade Capron suggested. "I knew his father. You can't blame the boy."

"Blame him for what?"

There was a moment's silence and then, "You know that we have some exceptional diamonds in the shop," Joseph Temple began. "A diamond from Temple and Peck—I sound like advertising copy. Bayne bought a stone from us a month ago. Sixteen thousand dollars. A square diamond. We mounted it in platinum. He gave it to Louise Harwood for an engagement ring. Peck tried to sell him a smaller stone but nothing would satisfy love's young dream except the sixteen-thousand-dollar piece. He paid us two thousand dollars. Peck gave him a two-year credit on the balance. That partner of mine is a fool. I'll let Meade Capron tell you the rest of the story."

The elderly Mr. Capron bathed his tonsils in a generous libation of thirty-year-old bourbon, coughed once and took the spotlight.

"It happens, Mr. Lee, that I am not unfamiliar with gem stones. Mr. Temple will tell you...."

"Capron knows emeralds," Joseph Temple interrupted. "He knows as much about emeralds as any man in the country. He knows enough about diamonds for our present purposes."

Old Meade Capron frowned for a moment at the limitations set upon the compliment and then, "I saw the square diamond the day after young Bayne gave it to Louise Harwood. I had seen it several times before. It is a distinguished stone. I saw Miss Harwood again yesterday evening at her mother's house. She was wearing the ring, but the square diamond had been replaced. Paste! The imitation would pass well enough with the average observer—under electric lights. I kept my counsel. You and Mr. Temple know of my discovery. No one else."

"Didn't you speak of the substitution to Miss Harwood?" James Lee queried.

"For obvious reasons I did not. I went so far as to suggest that the ring's romantic associations must impel her to wear it day and night." At this point old Meade Capron snorted his opinion of the younger generation. "She assured me that its romantic value was zero. She confessed that she laid it aside with her other jewelry every night. More important—she told me that she had entrusted the stone to young Warren Bayne for two days. The ring was slightly large for her finger. She and Bayne and a dozen other wild young people had gone to Hollywood on a party with some movie people whom they met at Del Monte. She is..."

"Is Miss Harwood addicted to wild parties?"

Old Meade Capron fortified his spirit with another shot of bourbon before he permitted himself to answer. "She is the wildest girl in her set. She is..."

"That's not the point," Joseph Temple interrupted. The jeweler, sticking close to his indictment of Warren Bayne, let the case against Louise Harwood rest in his eagerness to present the evidence against the young man. "Actually we're not much interested in the girl," he said. "She's a wild young fool but Bayne is a wild young crook. He's a flashy ne'er-do-well. He never did a day's work in his life unless you call polo work. He's notoriously a heavy gambler and notoriously a loser. He has no income. He's always broke. He's been in trouble over his bank account a hundred times. He's marrying Louise Harwood for her money."

“Her mother's money,” Meade Capron interposed.

“Her mother's money,” Joseph Temple admitted. “And now, needing cash, he virtually steals a diamond from the girl he's engaged to marry!”

James Lee's eyes narrowed. “That's a fairly strong statement.”

“I admit it. It can't be strong enough to...”

“You've left out the important fact,” Meade Capron interposed. “Tell Mr. Lee about Warren Bayne's bank account.”

Joseph Temple nodded violently. “The bank account! That's the whole story!” he exploded. “I was leading up to it. Listen to this! The day after Warren Bayne got back from the Hollywood orgy and got sobered up he deposited six thousand dollars in the West National. Was it a check? It was not! Was it a draft to his order? It was not! The money was in cash!” In his rage Joseph Temple glared at James Lee. “Cash that he got from some pawnbroker, some fence in payment for my diamond!”

“How did you learn about the six thousand?”

“Confidential information from the cashier of the West National. He's a friend of mine.”

James Lee waited for a moment and then: “I'd say your next move is to swear out a warrant for the young man. What do you want me to do?—unofficially. The Department of Justice isn't interested in such things.”

“Swear out a warrant!” Joseph Temple scowled in helpless rage. “Do you know what that means? We don't swear out warrants for the damned polo set. It would cost me fifty important customers—very important customers—the day the news was published.”

“I still fail to see where I draw any cards in this game.” Lee frowned at Joseph Temple. “What do you want me to do?”

“The case is clear enough against young Bayne. As long as you're professionally associated with crime and criminals you can settle this affair without any publicity. Get hold of Bayne and tell him for me that if he pays over the six thousand dollars that he has in the West National I will let the balance ride for a while. You can suggest that if he does not turn the six thousand over to us we will sock him with a warrant.”

After a moment, “It's thin material to high-jack a man with,” Lee suggested. “What else have you got on young Bayne? We need something more definite than your suspicions.”

With rising temper, “He's a rotter!” Mr. Temple exploded. “Notorious for his drunken parties. You can scare him with that mess he got into at Braga's gambling joint after the Stanford game. Louise Harwood and a dozen of her friends were in the party. If Braga's bartender had died it would have been manslaughter.”

Lee shook his head. “That's a little bit vague. Everybody gets into messes after football games. Help yourself to the sherry and cool off.”

Under the soothing influence of this third glass of sherry, “You'd better come home to dinner with me,” Mr. Temple said. “We can talk this out.”

“Thank you, not this evening. I'll stay here and do a little quiet thinking.”

Mr. Temple brightened. “You mean you'll work on this diamond job?”

James Lee nodded.

“Yes,” he said. “Please don't do anything... violent until you hear from me.”

When his visitors had left, James Lee walked to the kitchen of his apartment. Facing his Chinese cook, “Do you know the servants in Mrs. Rockwell Harwood's house?” he asked.

“Missy Harwood cook long time my friend. He my cousin.”

“Mrs. Harwood's daughter has a big diamond ring. She is to marry young Mr. Warren Bayne. He gave her the ring.”

“I know him. Very wild boy, fight likee soldier.”

James Lee nodded in full agreement with his cook's opinion of Warren Bayne. “I want to see Miss Harwood's diamond. Ask your cousin to get hold of the ring. Tell him to bring it down here tonight.”

“Mebbe no can do.”

“Maybe can do. Try it.”

“If can do he ketchum....”

After he had enjoyed his dinner James Lee smoked a cigarette leisurely in the quiet of his library. When the cigarette was finished he put a call through the Chinatown Exchange, cackling a demand in Cantonese for a number that did not answer until central had rung three times.

To the reluctant "Hola" of a thin voice that answered him, "Put Chin Yut on the line," James Lee demanded.

"Chin Yut long time go way."

"This is James Lee speaking. Put Chin Yut on the line."

"Chin Yut is speaking."

"Come to my house at once."

"I come now." A click ended the evidence of Chin Yut's bending will.

Facing Chin Yut without further preliminary than a nod of greeting, "You are acquainted with the gambling house run by Braga Covilla?" James Lee asked.

For an instant a grimace of amusement distorted Chin Yut's cadaverous countenance. "Who is not?"

"He is still a customer of yours?"

When Chin Yut hesitated with his reply, "I have the records on Braga's purchases, complete," James Lee added.

A mask of rage replaced the smile on Chin Yut's face. "I must kill a man or two in my employ," he said.

"You have some good men in your employ. Answer me! Braga still buys opium from you?"

Chin Yut nodded his head. "You know that he does," he said sullenly.

"How many smoking-rooms has he in his gambling house?"

"He has three rooms."

"For white men?"

"For white men and white women," Chin Yut answered. "He serves no others."

"That's all," James Lee said. "Chin Yut, your feet are on the pathway to hell."

"That is evidently a secret known to the world. Good luck, long life."

"Sons to mourn at your grave," James Lee said, following the Ritual of Right Conduct. "Good night."

When Chin Yut had left his apartment, James Lee summoned his house boy. "Mrs. Harwood's cook will probably come to see me tonight. Admit him instantly. I am going to sleep now. You stay awake."

The genius of the kitchen in the Harwood home rang the bell of James Lee's apartment two hours after midnight.

The house boy ushered him into the library of the apartment. "My master will welcome you in one moment," he said.

When he had greeted his visitor, "The daughter of your house is—careless with her treasures?" James Lee asked.

In answer the Harwood cook hauled a knotted silk handkerchief out of the depths of an inner pocket of his coat. "This is the ring," he said.

When he had removed the silk covering from the ring James Lee observed the stone for a moment, flooding it with the strong greenish light of one of the reading lamps in the library. He turned to the house boy. "Serve our guest with whatever refreshments he may desire," he ordered, and then to the Harwood cook, "If you will excuse me I will return in a few moments."

In a long inside room of his apartment which had been fitted up as a laboratory James Lee devoted ten minutes to an accurately checked measurement of the refractive index of the stone in Louise Harwood's ring. Presently, averaging the six readings that he had made, confirming old Meade Capron's opinion of the stone, "Strass," he decided. "One, point nine seven five."

For a moment following his measurement of the refractive index of the false gem he considered making a test for its specific gravity. Then, "Difficult—and nothing much to be gained by it," he decided. "We win or lose on one, point nine seven five."

He returned to his library, where his guest awaited him. He handed the ring to Mrs. Harwood's cook. "You have served me well. Let me know when I may express my gratitude more effectively," he said. "A cup of wine?... Plenteous years."

Choking slightly over the bourbon which he had selected in preference to the sherry on the library table, "Seven sons at thy grave," the cook complimented.

"And silence."

The cook bowed to James Lee. "A wise man understands a nod."

When his visitor had gone James Lee went to bed without delay. "I shall want nothing more tonight," he said to his house boy who stood waiting in his master's bedroom. "Breakfast at seven. I have a busy day planned for tomorrow. Call me at six-thirty."

Of the six facet-cutting machines in San Francisco two belonged to private owners and four to lapidaries who did commercial work. It was two o'clock in the afternoon before James Lee finished his interview with the man who operated the fourth of these commercial machines.

Returning to his apartment he telephoned a brief message to Louise Harwood. "I should like to have you call at my apartment," he said. "This is James Lee, Department of Justice, speaking."

After a moment, "I will come," the girl faltered.

"At four o'clock?"

"At four o'clock."

When he had given Louise Harwood his address James Lee hung up the telephone.

To his house boy a moment later, "A lady will call here to see me at four o'clock," he said. "I will receive her in the library. In the meantime go down to the Twin Pigeon Jewelry Store—present my compliments to Moy Sam and tell him that I have need of his services this afternoon. Ask him to be here at four o'clock. Entertain him in your room until I summon him."

Promptly at four o'clock, impelled by a growing fear of the threat that she had read into James Lee's invitation, Louise Harwood rang the bell of Lee's apartment.

Greeting Louise Harwood, "First of all, let me assure you that you will not regret this visit," James Lee said to the frightened girl. "You are unhappy now. On my word of honor you will leave here presently with your heart lightened of its burden—and with your Braga problem solved. The opium..."

"I did not smoke any opium...."

James Lee lifted his hand. "I know that," he said. "I also know the names of your three companions who did—three young ladies. They were prompted by the mystery and the novelty of the thing, no doubt—but one of them is by way of becoming an addict now."

The look of surprise on Louise Harwood's face gave way to horror.

"Do you mean that she..."

Interrupting the girl, "She has will enough to save herself."

After a moment of silence, "I should like to have you come into my laboratory for a little while."

From an open box that sat on a table against the west wall of his laboratory James Lee lifted out a handful of glittering crystals. "Here is a beautiful piece of amethyst," he said, holding a purple crystal to the light. "And some rose quartz.... These are emeralds. Beautiful enough but of no value.... This is a piece of glass. Do you remember from your school days how these things are identified—their relative hardness, their specific gravity, their varying abilities to bend a ray of light? This beautiful substance is glass—do you see how its prisms break up the light into the spectrum colors? What a pure blue!... Have you ever seen a ray of sunlight after it has been passed through a prism?"

"We had a lot of those things in school," Louise Harwood said. "I didn't pay much attention to them."

James Lee smiled. "A ray of sunlight is not very interesting when one is—in school." He turned the prismatic piece of glass in his hand until one of its facets glowed with a brilliant orange light. "This is a very beautiful gem," he said. "Worth a dollar of any debased currency. I will show you how we determine its refractive index.... See, I fix it in this machine and now through this prismatic section of the stone I direct... this pencil of light.... This is a beautiful machine. Reading direct... and we read on the scale one, point nine seven five. That is the refractive index of this glass. It is, by the way, the heaviest flint glass that I have ever seen. Here is a crystal of quartz. It is much harder than glass but its refractive index is considerably less than the glass we have just tested.... Do you find that this pastime bores you?"

The girl smiled a thin smile. "It is all very interesting," she said languidly.

"It will become more interesting perhaps," James Lee suggested. From a closed drawer to his right he removed another complex, glittering crystal. "This is another substance—pure carbon. The glass was principally silica and potash and lead. The refractive index of this carbon crystal is much higher than the glass. You see it reads around two, point four two—a little less perhaps. This stone is called a diamond. The origin of the word is lost in antiquity. The Arabs and the Greeks and Romans had it 'adamas'—unconquerable. This is a very beautiful stone, by the way. Strangely enough it seems to be a replica of the stone you are wearing. May I see your ring a moment?"

Louise Harwood held her hand out toward James Lee. "I can't get it off my finger. The ring is too small."

"Perhaps if we moistened your finger with a drop of glycerine.... There. Now it comes off. Now let us fix it in this machine and... That's surprising, isn't it? The glass in your ring has the same refractive index as the lead glass we examined a few moments ago. What a coincidence. One, point nine seven five. It is really a first-rate imitation of a diamond. I suppose you leave your real jewels in the safe-deposit vaults?"

"It's the safest way," the girl faltered inanely.

"Quite." James Lee nodded in quick agreement to this and then, "Isn't it strange that the difference in value between this diamond here in front of you and that piece of glass in your ring should be fifteen or twenty thousand dollars? Certainly the price of a diamond is no index of its beauty.... But wouldn't you rather have this real diamond than that piece of glass? It's a marvelous gem."

Without waiting for the girl to reply James Lee called abruptly to his house boy: "Please tell Moy Sam to come in here a moment."

When the Chinese jeweler stood before him, James Lee handed him Louise Harwood's ring. "Take that piece of glass out of the ring," he directed. "Substitute this diamond in place of it. You will find that the setting fits the diamond."

Lee turned to the girl quickly and held out an open cigarette case. "Have a cigarette," he said. "Enjoy the rich blessing of tobacco while Moy Sam does his work. He is very skillful.... See there, how perfectly the diamond fits your ring?"

Three minutes later when Louise Harwood had returned the ring to her finger and when they were again alone, "You may cry now for sixty seconds," James Lee suggested to her.

Presently, after the girl had devoted something more than sixty seconds to her tears, James Lee picked up the glass crystal that Moy Sam had taken from the ring. "Strangely enough," he said, "Braga Covilla gave the order for the manufacture of that imitation of your diamond. I found the man who cut this piece of glass—and he named his customer. I pried the story and the diamond out of Braga on the strength of what I know about his opium business. Let me wrap that glass gem up for you. Take it with you for good luck."

James Lee reached for a blue slip of paper that lay in the drawer of his work table. He held the slip of paper toward Louise Harwood. "You have seen this before? It is the check that you gave Braga the afternoon you entertained so lavishly—and lost so heavily at roulette. Here, I will wrap your glass gem in it—and that makes your souvenir of this visit to my house complete."

Now for twice sixty seconds the girl's voice came through incoherent sobs. When she was quieter, "I did not know—the penalty—for forgery—until Braga spoke of the penitentiary. He threatened me. I gave him the diamond. Overdrafts were nothing. I always got money from Mother. I'd lost a lot of money at roulette and I was full of cocktails."

"Not a very good defense when a blackmailer is after you," James Lee interrupted. "May I offer you a glass of sherry?... Let us sink this whole affair out of memory. Braga will keep his mouth shut. I forget easily and completely." To his conscience, "Once more I have compounded a felony!"

James Lee lifted his glass of wine toward Louise Harwood. "I wish you a happy wedding and a happy honeymoon with Mr. Warren Bayne."

Through her quiet tears, "You have made it possible for life to be happy for me," the girl whispered. "I cannot express my gratitude, Mr. Lee—and oh, I'll never forget how darned wonderful you've been."

After Louise Harwood had left his apartment, James Lee rang through on the telephone for Joseph Temple. "I've made a little progress," he reported when Mr. Temple answered.

"I knew you would! Is that rascal going to turn over the six thousand dollars to us?"

"I'd go easy on the 'that rascal' as you call him. The six thousand is his commission on the sale of a Monterey ranch that he induced one of his big-shot movie friends to buy. He's going to spend it all on his honeymoon trip. You'd better lay off the six thousand."

"But what about the diamond?"

“Miss Harwood is wearing the diamond,” James Lee announced. “If I were you I'd advise old Meade Capron to have his eyes examined.”

“Are you sure?”

“Perfectly sure. The lights in the Harwood house may have deceived Mr. Capron. You never can tell what a ray of light will do. Maybe any engagement ring looks phony to a man as old as Meade Capron.”

THE BELL FROM CHINA

Fang Man was fat, and his smile was worth big money to the Gold Tiger Company. Casual customers who visited the store on Gamblers' Alley in San Francisco believed that Fang Man owned the Gold Tiger outfit. As a matter of fact, he owned three shares, of eighty, but he wore the mantle of authority in a manner that gave reason for the public's error. Most of the stock in the Gold Tiger was the common merchandise of Chinatown, but enough good stuff drifted in from China to make the place good hunting for collectors of the best things in Chinese art. Mr. Arnold Fisher, a director of the Pacific Art League, was one of Fang Man's most constant visitors. A recognized authority on design and color, Mr. Fisher's hobby was Chinese art. As a collector his activities were limited by a very modest income but he had a genius for engineering contributions to the Art League's collection and not many of the finer things that turned up in Fang Man's importations escaped him.

Wealthy old girls and boys, observing the distinguished artist's sincere conniption fits at the sight of a really fine piece of jade or bronze or pottery, would often buy it forthwith to save Mr. Fisher's life. Mr. Fisher would accept the purchase for the Art League's collection and go to dinner with his glowing patron, ushered to the door of the Gold Tiger by the beaming Fang Man and the full company of cackling clerks that staffed the pungent shop.

Eight clerks, a cashier and Fang Man. Rent and salaries. A lot of overhead—but nobody ever gave that a thought because the Gold Tiger was seemingly big enough to support ten or fifteen people, China fashion, and the public knew nothing at all about the seventy-seven shares in the enterprise that were held by Fang Man's various partners. The Gold Tiger shares were worth five thousand dollars apiece and that was something else the public did not know. The annual dividend, the division of the profits in the first days of the First Moon—but that can wait while Fang Man introduces Arnold Fisher to James Lee: "Mistah Lee—Mistah Filly-shah. Him good man."

Fisher held out his hand. "I'm Arnold Fisher," he said, "of the Art League."

"I'm glad to meet you," James Lee said. "I know your Color Harmony—good book."

"Thank you. Are you a collector, Mr. Lee? Chinese art, I mean?"

"Him gup-ment man," the smiling Fang explained. "Large G-man. Good job fo' China man. Big money, him ketchum."

Lee frowned at Fang. "I have some early bronzes, and some jade," he said to Fisher. "Then there are some clay figures, too."

"Have you seen the Art League collection?"

"Yes. Some fine things there."

"Have you seen the bell and the two caldrons of the Chou Dynasty that we got last month?"

"No. I must see them."

"Perfect things!" Fisher's enthusiasm was manifest. "Magnificent stuff! The bell has a long inscription. Seventy or eighty characters. Can you translate the Chou inscriptions, Mr. Lee?"

"Without much difficulty."

"The reason I ask is that Dr. Call, of the university, is away for six months. He always does that work for us."

"No better man for the job," James Lee said. "He's the final authority."

"I'm awfully anxious to have the bell inscription worked out. Do you suppose you could find time to give us a general idea about it—date the bell, perhaps?"

"I think so. I'll be glad to try it. You know, of course, that there are fifty people in San Francisco who can work out those Chou inscriptions?"

"I know—and they'd give me fifty different translations. Some of them literally accurate, perhaps—but you will admit, Mr. Lee, that most of our local Chinese scholars are a bit vague with English."

"I understand. Sometimes it's difficult to express the essence of the Chinese mind in other languages."

"Exactly!... When do you think you can look at the bell? Work on the inscription, I mean?"

"This evening is free."

"Perfect! Will you come down to the League—or may I bring the bell to your house?"-

"My apartment is more convenient," James Lee said. "The bell probably weighs less than some of the reference books I'll use. Shall we say eight o'clock?"

"Good. I'll go down now and get the bell before the janitors lock up."

"Here is my address," James Lee said.

After Arnold Fisher had left, James Lee resumed his interrupted conversation with Fang Man. "I will not waste our time," he said in Cantonese, "by offering you the lead of advice. I suggest that you spend the gold of clear-seeing to purchase right conduct. Feet leaving Middle Pathway walk to gates of prison."

"Eyes of lion not seeing now?"

"Seeing well enough. Not blind when looking at your seven partners in Shanghai. One word to wise man better than ten thousand to fool. Word is—stop!"

Fang Man hesitated for three seconds. Blandly then, "Who am I to question the will of heaven?"

Within six hours a cablegram in code halted a shipment of opium whose sale in the United States would have meant two hundred thousand dollars for the Gold Tiger crew. Before the message reached Shanghai, James Lee was busy in his library with the difficult inscription on the bell of the Chou Dynasty that Arnold Fisher had brought in from the Art League collection.

"This is a tough one," James Lee said, after a preliminary inspection.

"I'm afraid I've imposed on you with a bigger job than you anticipated."

"Not at all," James Lee protested; "I enjoy it—only it really will take considerable time. Where, by the way, did you get it?"

"Fang Man imported it. Boad Hagardt presented it to the Art League. Do you know him?"

"I don't know him," James Lee said. "Let's see if we can find a date here."

"It's all a puzzle to me."

"No doubt. Here's something that may help us. Roughly 'Emperor nine moon ten seven year.' What emperor? This symbol can mean jade or king or great... four hands united.... Kung! I've got it! The emperor is Kung Wang! Now if the text describes some of his activities the piece can be an important find, historically. It can be terribly valuable!"

"It cost enough," Fisher observed.

James Lee frowned. "I wasn't thinking of its value in cash. What did Fang Man get for it?"

"Hagardt paid him two thousand."

"Mr. Hagardt is a handy man for the Art League to have around. Hang onto him."

"No fear. He's doing the hanging on. Wants to be just one of us humble seekers after beauty."

"Beauties, maybe? There are some lovely ladies in the art classes."

"He's all set that way. His wife is a knockout. Russian girl about half his age—with absolutely everything."

"I'll have this bell job worked out in a week or so." James Lee smiled. "It will be safe here."

Arnold Fisher blinked. "Oh, yes—the bell. Take all the time you want, Mr. Lee. By the way—of course you're coming to the Four Arts affair next month? Mrs. Hagardt is to be the Chinese empress. It's Chinese this year, as you probably know."

"Very happy to come. Your Javanese pageant last year was very colorful."

"This Chinese affair will be ten times as beautiful. I'll see that the committee reserves a box for you and your guests. And will you let me know when you get the bell puzzle solved?"

"Surely. I'll telephone. If I find anything really startling you'll get a progress report from me. Do we wear costume—in the boxes?"

"Yes. You'll see some pearls in the show. Costumes and acts and chorus groups solid with pearls."

"Nothing more spectacular—if it is properly lighted. Your idea?"

"Boad Hagardt sold me the pearl idea."

At the doorway of James Lee's apartment Arnold Fisher halted for a moment. "If that bell really does turn out to be an exceptional piece," he said, "maybe it would be a good idea not to let Fang Man know too much about it. He's an avaricious bird. He soaked Hagardt the full retail rate on a wholesale lot of pearl-embroidered costumes for the royal attendants in spite of his protested friendship."

"Why didn't you side-step and try the next bazaar?"

"Hagardt was the fall guy—sort of running that part of the show because Vera—Mrs. Hagardt—is the splendiferous empress. He's buying the costumes for the big act."

"I see. Who is playing the emperor's part?"

"I am."

James Lee bowed low to his departing guest. "Your most humble subject wishes you ten thousand years of felicity. See you soon again."

Returning to his problem of the inscription on the bell, James Lee was vaguely annoyed with some undefined element of the puzzle. Through long experience he had learned to discard wishful thinking in these matters and to trust his instinct rather than superficial evidence. Half consciously, absorbed in eager anticipation of what the cryptic text might reveal, "ninth moon, seventeenth year of the Emperor Kung Wang," he repeated.

Presently, basing his preliminary opinion on several intelligible phrases, "This is a proclamation of sovereignty over a new and vast domain," he decided. "Black night forests of five-needle pines in the north to almond-blooming third moon kingdom South," he quoted. Suddenly, "Almonds!" he exclaimed. Then, in the Occidental vernacular, "Nuts!" He reached out for a dictionary on the table to his right. After a moment, "Phonetically exact transcription of the Persian term," he decided. "Chinese 'Bwa-dam,' Middle Persian 'va-dam,' Persian 'badam'—meaning nuts to you, Mr. Fisher, and Mr. Boad Hagardt, and Mr. Fang Man!"

After a moment he laid the heavy bronze bell on its side. He walked into his laboratory, which adjoined his library, and returned with a hand drill. From a bright spot on the lip of the bell where the patina had been abraded he drilled a thin spiral of bronze. "Two strikes so far. Let's see what an assay for zinc and lead will show."

The careless manner in which he swung the heavy bell from the library table to the floor was in marked contrast to the careful handling that he had given it up to that moment. He summoned his houseboy. "Lock this away in the big vault with the other junk," he directed. Then, remembering an earlier thrill that the bell had inspired, “Handle it with care,” he said. “It's a good piece of work—of its kind.”

The Art League ball hit a new high for beauty and color long before the formal pageantry of the court scenes of the Manchu rulers replaced the throng of costumed dancers. At midnight the floor was cleared for the March of the Emperors and a brilliant tide of Oriental splendor flowed in from the costume rooms that flanked the vast arena.

Seated on their jeweled thrones, borne high by a hundred royal servants, Arnold Fisher and Vera Hagardt, clad in shimmering costumes embroidered with gold and pearls came on to face a barrage of flashlights and to be greeted with a roaring tempest of applause from the boxes and galleries.

Under the tumult James Lee became suddenly aware of a man's voice addressing him. “I'm Boad Hagardt,” the man said. “Arnold Fisher wanted me to meet you. Splendid show, isn't it?”

“Magnificent,” James Lee agreed. “Your wife is a very beautiful empress.”

Hagardt smiled. “She is a beautiful woman. You must meet her after—after she awakens from this dream.”

“I will be very happy to meet her,” James Lee said. Abruptly then, “The bronze bell of the Chou Dynasty that you donated to the Art League collection—may I ask where you found it?”

Hagardt hesitated for a moment and then, “I picked it up in Shanghai,” he said. “I bought it from one of you* million cousins, Lee Wing Chang, at the Three Sword Shop. Do you know him?”

Reading a mild irony in Hagardt's question, James Lee smiled thinly. “There are several million members of my family whom I have not met.... May I offer you a cigarette?”

“Thank you. What do you think of the bell?”

“A very interesting piece. Fang Man imported it for you?”

“What do you mean?”

“Fisher said you bought it from Fang Man.”

Hagardt nodded. “He's right. Those shops handle the customs men more easily than I can. You know all of the tiresome routine, I suppose.”

“I know some of it.”

"Silly business, isn't it? Takes you longer to get a piece through the customhouse than it does to get it across the Pacific. Can you read those old inscriptions, Mr. Lee?"

"With difficulty," James Lee said. And then, "I believe our heaven-born of ancient dynasties are returning to earth. Shall we try to find Fisher and your wife?"

"They will come here," Hagardt said. "Vera wants to meet you. Fisher told her you had translated the inscription on the bell. She is interested."

Within the hour James Lee had enjoyed two dances with Vera Hagardt. She was slender and her hands and feet were small. "Mixed blood in this girl's lineage," James Lee decided. Her eyes confirmed this. They were wide apart and large but a sinister fire glinted in their molten green. An aura of some exotic scent surrounded the woman.

Following their second dance, Vera Hagardt asked, over a glass of champagne, "Did you complete your translation of the inscription on the bell?"

"Not yet," James Lee said. "I find it quite difficult."

Vera Hagardt smiled. "Sometimes they don't make sense, do they?... Won't you have a cigarette, Mr. Lee?"

"Thank you, I have one."

"Won't you try one of mine?"

From the silver cigarette case that Vera Hagardt opened, James Lee selected a cigarette. He lighted it. "This is good," he said. "The Nandyal district?" Vera nodded. "You have a very acute sense of taste. A little farther south—three or four hundred miles, I believe. Dindigul."

"You have lived there?"

"No, but Mr. Hagardt lived there a year or two."

"He exhibits excellent taste in various things," James Lee said cryptically. "Incidentally, there he is—with Mr. Fisher. May I surrender custody of the heaven-born to the emperor and his companion? I'm not really old-fashioned about my bedtime but I have a lot of work to do tomorrow."

Vera Hagardt smiled her sweetest smile. "I hope I shall see you again, Mr. Lee. I have enjoyed meeting you."

After a moment with Hagardt and Arnold Fisher, James Lee bade them good night. On his way out of the auditorium, crossing the vast arena of the dance floor whereon some hundred revelers were hard at work making merry, he saw a dozen pearls that had been torn from one of the royal costumes. He picked up four of the pearls and put them into his pocket.

In his apartment, preparing for bed, James Lee questioned his servant, a Shanghai man, about the Three Sword Shop from which the bronze bell had come. "I seem to remember that Lee Wing Chang is a man of evil."

The servant bowed. "My master is of clear perception. For twenty years Lee Wing Chang has notoriously been associated with evil enterprise."

"Thank you; that is all," James Lee said, and added, "A man can dig his own grave with his tongue."

At eleven o'clock the next day James Lee telephoned Arnold Fisher. "I'd like to see you some time this afternoon if it is convenient."

"Any hour you name. I'll be in my studio all day."

"Recovering from the party?"

"I'm afraid it will take more than one day," Fisher said. "I drank too much champagne. By the way, do you know Fang Man very well?"

"Fairly well," James Lee said. "What about him?"

"He sent a messenger up here for that emperor's costume that I wore. I'd like to keep it but the Chinese that came for it was quite insistent."

"Did you give it to him?"

"No. I wonder if you can make some arrangement with Fang Man so I can buy it from him."

"I thought Hagardt bought those costumes."

"The Chinaman said that Fang Man had bought them back from Hagardt."

"Why didn't you telephone Hagardt about it?"

"I called him but he wasn't in."

"I'll see if I can fix it up for you. I'll see you about five o'clock in your studio. May I bring you some first aid—the hair of the dog that bit you?"

"No, thanks. I think I'll live."

Arnold Fisher thought that he would live, but in this he was wrong. At five o'clock, when James Lee rang the bell at the door of Fisher's studio, there was no answer. He opened the door. "Hello, Fisher," he called. "Where are you? Sleeping it off?" Then, looking down, he saw Fisher, face down on the floor back of the long couch that fronted the fireplace. Fisher was in his pajamas and he wore a voluminous dressing gown of vermilion silk. He was dead from a shot through his heart. A pool of blood lay under his chest and his body was still warm.

"Killed within the last hour," James Lee decided. He devoted the next ten minutes to a quick examination of Fisher's studio and the other rooms of his apartment. The pearl-embroidered costume was missing. He went to the telephone then and called his office. Frank Wilbur answered him.

"James Lee speaking. Is Riley there?"

"Right here."

"Turn the office over to Sabin or Parrish. I want you and Riley to meet me at my apartment right away."

"Okay. Be there in five minutes."

In his library, to Riley and Wilbur: "Arnold Fisher was murdered at his studio less than an hour ago. Director of the Pacific Art League. Wilbur, you go down in Gamblers' Alley and round up Fang Man. Hold everybody in the joint. Riley, you're coming with me. I'm making a call on Boad Hagardt and his wife. Did you see her picture in the morning papers?"

Riley nodded. "Some swell dame," he commented. "What's the play?"

"You and I will go to Hagardt's house in my car. Wilbur, you'd better get some help on your Fang Man job. In about half an hour tell one of the cops to notify the homicide squad that Fisher is dead in his studio. I didn't report the murder because I need a little time on the Hagardt angle."

"Do we hold Fang Man on a murder charge?" Frank Wilbur asked.

"I'm not sure yet," James Lee said. "One of Fang Man's crew may have shot Fisher. Ask the coroner not to touch Fisher's body until I get another look at it."

"Okay. Is that all?"

"That's all. Hop to it!"

James Lee opened the upper left-hand drawer of his library desk. From an open cardboard box he selected two of the four pearls that he had found on the dance floor at the Art League ball. He handed one of these to Riley. "Come into the shop," he said. "Try this in a test tube with strong nitric acid. If she comes orange-red and changes to yellow we've got something."

In his laboratory James Lee laid the second pearl in a concave disk of glass. He mixed three cubic centimeters of strong sulphuric acid with a forty-percent formaldehyde solution and submerged the pearl in the mixture. A purple-red coloration resulted which presently changed to violet and then to blue.

"We have something!" he said to Riley. "What happened with the nitric acid?"

"Look," Riley said. "Orange-red. Just what have we got?"

"We have a hot trail. Are you wearing your guns?"

"Only a small automatic."

"Get a big one from the desk in the library. Upper right-hand drawer. Come along."

In the car, en route to Boad Hagardt's house, "Give me three minutes and then follow me in," James Lee directed. "Blast your way in if you have to. Three minutes, no more, no less."

"Okay," Riley said, "three minutes."

James Lee stopped his car a block from Boad Hagardt's house. The front door was opened ten seconds after James Lee rang the bell. Boad Hagardt himself bowed to his visitor.

"How do you do, Mr. Lee? Come in. How are you?"

"Quite well, thank you," James Lee said; "just a bit nervous."

"Not enough sleep last night?"

"Plenty of sleep. I'm a bit nervous about that gun in your right coat packet. Or is it a gun?"

Instantly the lines about Boad Hagardt's mouth deepened. "Yes, it's a gun," he grated. "What about it? Come in here." Boad Hagardt's scowl changed to a sneer. "Come in and meet the family."

"Thank you," James Lee said. "I'd be very happy to see Mrs. Hagardt."

Hagardt called over his shoulder to his wife, "Vera! Your Chink friend wants to see you. Are you receiving?"

From the living room, twenty feet down the hall, Vera Hagardt answered her husband: “If it's Mr. James Lee by any chance I'd be delighted to meet him.”

“Get in there.” Hagardt emphasized his order with an arrested gesture of the pistol in his right coat pocket.

James Lee walked down the hallway to the door of the living room. He paused a moment in the doorway, bowing to Vera Hagardt. “So happy to see you,” he said.

“The same to you,” the woman said, lapsing into a vernacular and a manner in strong contrast to her regal demeanor of the previous night. “You've got your nerve coming to this house.”

“Possibly.” James Lee smiled. “I see you've changed your shoes.”

“What do you mean?”

“Listen, Vera, frisk that guy,” Hagardt interposed. “I've got him covered.”

“Excuse me for being so personal, Mr. Lee,” Vera Hagardt said, hauling a forty-five automatic out of a holster against her guest's right hip pocket. “What do you mean about my shoes?” The woman laid the pistol on a table that stood in the center of the living room.

“The ones with the yellow clay on them. The yellow clay from the telephone company's conduit trench in front of your house. You left a bit of it on the rug in Arnold Fisher's studio this afternoon—and does your scalp hurt you? The little wound made by one of Fisher's fingernails? Eight or ten of your auburn hairs are missing. I'm afraid they won't grow back. You were careless, too, with the ashes from your cigarette. You might just as well have left your card. That Indian tobacco. The ash is so high in potassium chloride that it is unmistakable. And that exotic perfume you use—why did you kill Fisher?”

While James Lee spoke, fear, then absolute wide-eyed horror, replaced the thin mask of contempt on Vera Hagardt's face. She turned to her husband.

“Bump him, now. Bump him! Don't let him talk that way to me,” she cried.

Boad Hagardt nodded. “I'll bump him soon enough. I'll bump you, Lee—and you'll go into the bay tonight feet first. What the hell are you messing into my game for?”

"That's my business," James Lee said easily. "Bump and be damned, Hagardt! You lose either way. Patron of the arts! Donor of bronze bells! Almonds in the reign of Kung Wang! You fool—almonds weren't known in China for five hundred years after that emperor died. Seventeenth year of the emperor's reign. Not a trace of zinc or lead. Even the alloy was phony. Too bad you had it cast in Wing Chang's shop across the street from the biggest morphine factory in South China. Neighbors! Pearls! You stood to make half a million on this job, didn't you, Hagardt? A hundred coats, embroidered solid with pearls. Two or three million morphine pills! You stood to make some big dough. Slick trick, but you didn't get away with it."

"Don't kid yourself," Hagardt snarled; "we'll get away with it! We'll get away with you, too, like we got away with Fisher. Put that in your pipe and drag deep! How'd you like to have a couple of those pills right now?"

"I have a couple of them left, thank you," James Lee said. "I've used two of them in test tubes. They're morphine. Your wife killed poor Fisher because he blocked your game by holding out one coat!"

"What of it? The dope's in circulation and you're out of the picture. Not quite out but you're on your way. Fang Man said you were a slick Chink. You're slick, all right!"

The crash of a pistol shot echoed down the hallway from where Riley had fired his forty-five through the lock on the front door. Boad Hagardt turned toward the door of the living room. From where he stood James Lee leaped for the gun that lay on the table. His right hand slashed down and closed on the gun. In the next second he fired twice at Hagardt.

The first shot ripped through Hagardt's throat. The second one, superfluous, got the falling man through the heart. Hagardt was dead when he hit the floor. By the time Riley came through the door James Lee had swung his weapon in a line direct for Vera Hagardt's heart. "Get the links on that woman," he said. "Here! Here's another pair. Clip her ankles.... Thanks. Now get on the phone and tell the police department that we have caught a couple of killers. Hop to it. I want to get down and see how Wilbur came out with the Fang Man mob."

James Lee turned to Vera Hagardt. He lighted a cigarette for the woman and handed it to her. “Not your favorite Indian tobacco,” he suggested—“but better than nothing.”

THE FEAST OF KALI

On Monday after Denman Hale had paid him his July wages, old Chew Lim decided to enjoy a night out. Over the weekend the big house on Hale Island had been the scene of high-pressure festivities and now that his master's guests had gone Chew Lim was fed up with the whirl of California hospitality.

"Why fo' allee time you ketchum too many people you' house?" he complained, parking the currency that Denman Hale dealt out to him. "Mo' bettah Sabbaday, Sumday you set down sleepum lilly bit. Too large whoopee bad pidgin."

"Lissen, you desiccated old mummy, the whoopee business is my main dish," Hale announced. "Here, pay Tony this hundred bucks... and sixty for Bong Yut. I'm going to Stockton."

"You suppeh Stockton?"

"Yep, I suppose Stockton."

"Ai, no good! Stockton you dlink too muchee olo-fashion whiskee, play too many poker all night."

"Wrong again, you cackling conscience! I'm going to Stockton to make a deal with Pete Roncalo to fatten forty thousand lambs here on the island instead of starving them in the mountains."

"Where you makee lamb fat?"

"I'm going to run that mob of raghead Hindus out of that thousand-acre tract of sugar beets and plant it to Ladino clover. I win on that bet two for one—get rid of the rag-heads, get rid of the beets, and cash big on the lambs."

Old Chew Lim approved of this. "Good pidgin," he admitted. "Where you eat suppeh?"

Reading the Oriental mind, "I'm not going near the club," Hale said. "I'm having dinner with Pete and some of his Basque pals at Zaragoza's place—and it's too bad you can't cook as well as that Basque."

"Pah, he cookum too muchee pepper, eprything led hot.... Tonight I go see my cousin."

"Fair enough, but stay clear of Sang Hop's outfit. You go aboard of that ark boat and Sang Hop's gang would clean you in ten minutes."

"I savvy him." This with a finality that indicated a perfect immunity to the temptations of the wine and women and song purveyed by the notorious Sang Hop on board the Seaborn Heaven.

In the early evening, after Denman Hale had left for his meeting with Pete Roncalo, Chew Lim ate his supper with Tony Parente, the Hale gardener, and Bong Yut, the house-boy. After the meal was eaten he changed from his white uniform to a roomy gray suit that his master had discarded for O.D. in '17.

In this, with a flat-rimmed black sombrero riding his ears and with a corrugated pair of size-twelve black shoes on his number seven feet, he set out for China Camp on Beaver Island, five miles to the north, where Fish River marked the boundary of his master's land.

Halfway along his march, at the elbow in China Channel where Jordan Slough branched to the west, he scowled at the lighted windows of the Seaborn Heaven moored beneath the willows that fringed the south levee of Bent Island. Guitar music and the babble of a dozen tongues, laughter and the guttural supplication of the dice owner in a crap game, the strident clanking of a sick piano, and the clear, recurrent bells of three harmonizing cash registers. "Ai, tonight Sang Hop suffers no lack of victims.... Heaven is generous with this year's crop of fools!"

Chew Lim's opinion of the evil Sang Hop and his Seaborn Heaven was tempered with an easy tolerance not shared by his master. To Denham Hale, Chinese ark boats with their crooked women, their crooked gambling and their crooked hooch, were important contributors to his labor problems. They had functioned constructively, perhaps, through an earlier epoch when the army of laborers in the Delta had been recruited from the Chinese, but after the advent of companies of Japanese, Hindus, Mexicans and Filipinos the Seaborn Heaven and all similar craft at once became breeding spots of trouble—incubators of drunkenness, disease, violence and criminal enterprise ranging from minor racial conflicts to black murder.

"Ark boats be damned" was one of Denman Hale's more gentle generalities. Specifically with reference to Sang Hop and the proximate Seaborn Heaven, he had more than once deplored the rules and regulations that prohibited direct action in protecting his army of laborers. He had contemplated gunfire and arson and dynamite, but he had weakened under the white man's burden to where vituperative phrases and the lagging servants of the law, working with subsidized reluctance, were his only weapons.

Chew Lim, scowling at the Seaborn Heaven, turned his back on temptation and pursued his course to China Camp. Three miles of it, and then at Fish River he hailed his countrymen across the narrow channel. "Hola! The boatman!"

A voice, presently, in Cantonese, "Who calls?"

"Chew Lim. Make haste. I am weary."

In the dim interior of the main shack of China Camp, swamping his fatigue under generous splashes of potent black wine, Chew Lim relaxed and indulged himself in a gratifying exchange of garrulous gossip.

In the rosy glow of the warming wine, "We, my countrymen, are about to enjoy once more the smile of Milo Fo," he predicted. "Good years, plenteous blessings, the favor of Kwan Yin, will soon replace the barren deserts that we have known."

A chorus of skeptics answered him. "The vapors of strong drink cloud thy perception."

"I speak with reason," Chew Lim protested. "This day my master, who is prominent and powerful in this province, has ruled in our favor in two important instances. First of all, he has decided that men of China, sons of the Central Glory, will replace the despised laborers of India in the broad fields of his domain. In the second place he has decided to destroy our enemy, Sang Hop, his Seaborn Heaven and the evil robbers who infest the craft.... In the annals of our lives there are auspicious events. Hola! Let us drink to this great man whom I serve!"

Within the hour the evil Sang Hop, on board the Seaborn Heaven, had received a report of old Chew Lim's announcement.

Smiling blandly as he paid the informer with a handful of silver coins, "A stone lion does not fear the rain," Sang Hop observed. "I must put an end to these annoying attentions from the great Denman Hale."

Old Chew Lim had talked too much. Before midnight his announcement of Denman Hale's plans had been relayed to various interested proprietors of the underworld throughout the Delta and in Stockton.

When Denman Hale said good night to Pete Roncalo and various other Basques in Zaragoza's restaurant in Stockton, he started for his car, which was parked seventy feet from the entrance of the restaurant. Before he had covered half the distance two turbaned figures stepped to the sidewalk from the driver's seat of a dilapidated black touring car. They were beside Hale in three seconds. In the darkness one of the men raised his hand to launch a looped cord around Hale's throat.

The victim gave one futile gasp for air before consciousness left him. As he fell, one of the turbaned figures caught him and a moment later he was bundled into the tonneau of the touring car.

Old Chew Lim assuredly had talked too much. Ignorant of his error, still pleasantly inspired by the wine he had enjoyed in China Camp, Chew Lim halted at Jordan Slough on his return journey to Hale's house and again observed the lighted windows of the Seaborn Heaven. A pipe of good black opium, the hazard of a dollar or two at one of Sang Hop's fan-tan tables—why not? Momentary diversion, temporary freedom from the heavy burden of unceasing labor. Kwan Yin might smile upon the resourceful man, small fortune be the reward of action. If the dragon of chance devoured a bit of hard money, what of it?

At midnight, with a heavy purse and a light heart, Chew Lim edged into the packed throng at a fan-tan table, mumbled a prayer to Milo Fo, and risked the first dollar on a losing bet.

The rim of the world to the east was gray when Chew Lim stumbled ashore and resumed his return journey along the willow-fringed levee toward Denman Hale's house. His stomach burned with the acid dregs of raw wine, his flaming eyes were being ground to pulp against the serrated perimeter of a rotating earthquake that rumbled and screeched inside his skull, his tongue was a clacking cinder in the seething lava that lined his throat—and his purse was empty.

Southward along China Channel for two miles and then the level rays of the sun struck through his quivering eyelids with a fire that seemed to ignite his brain. For relief he kept his tortured eyes turned toward the quenching shadows under the drooping willows to his right. The little wavelets of the tidal current refreshed him with their insistent theme of desert springs. His eyes widened to the grateful shade and for a moment he was tempted to roll down the bank for a plunge into the cooling water.

Then, twenty feet below him, crumpled against the trunk of a willow tree, he saw the body of a man. The man's sightless eyes stared up at the shading leaves, and his swollen lips stretched wide in a grimace of death about his clenched teeth.

At the shock of discovery old Chew Lim whined softly for a moment under the lash of his nerves. After a while, by the force of his weakened will, he looked down once more at the dead man. Now, sure of the man's identity, he trembled at the realization of the grave portent of the tragedy. "Sang Hop was quick to strike!" Forthwith, in haste to quit the scene, he resumed his flight to sanctuary, ambling along the rutted roadway on the levee, in a palsy of fear, shaking in terror at a premonition of disasters yet to come.

It was nearly six when Chew Lim reached his master's house. He made his way at once to Denman Hale's bedroom. He knocked on the door, and again, more loudly, but there was no answering voice. Before he opened the door he knew with an absolute certainty that Denman Hale was not in the room. He entered the room. A quick inspection revealed no evidence that Denman Hale had returned from his supper engagement in Stockton with Pete Roncalo.

For a moment, "My fears for my master are groundless," he reflected. "I am the victim of my own senseless visionings." He remembered the dead man under the willows, and forthwith his fears were renewed. He knew that all the formal agencies of the law were powerless to halt the murder crew. With an inspiration born of his desperate need he thought of his countryman James Lee. "He is skilled in combat with the evil creatures of the white man's world. He knows the minds and methods of the criminal lords of the Central Glory. He alone can win against the killers that Sang Hop employs.... At this late moment he alone may save my master's life!"

He walked to the telephone at the head of Denman Hale's bed. The instrument trembled in his hands, but presently the call went through to James Lee in San Francisco. Abruptly after he had spoken his name, "Death rides this land," Chew Lim said, speaking his native Cantonese dialect. "Sang Hop's men have killed Lai Gulam, who rules the men of India for my master. It means that my master is in deadly peril. You must help me."

In his apartment in San Francisco, James Lee hesitated for five seconds. He made a quick summary of the official duties that filled the program of his day. Then, realizing the gravity of Chew Lim's statement, "I will come to you at once," he said. "Wait for me at your master's house. Until then, silence."

Denman Hale regained consciousness in a dilapidated frame house in Stockton to which his captors had conveyed him. His hands were bound behind him with a length of the cord with which his captors had strangled him. He discovered that his ankles were bound so tightly that all sensation had left his feet. A wad of cotton cloth had been stuffed into his mouth. His face lay against the moist earth floor of the room.

A faint light filled the room. The air of the place was foul with the moldy odor of wet earth mingled with the sickening fumes of heavy incense.

The prostrate man became vaguely aware, presently, of some activity behind him. He realized that two men were digging a pit in the earthen floor of the place. He attempted to move his head so that he might observe the scene, but he was too weak. He heard one of the men speak a dozen words of a Hindu jargon.

"We must dig the pit deeper," the man said. "Large bodies require deep graves."

A film of darkness veiled Denman Hale's eyes as merciful unconsciousness returned.

When James Lee's car roared across the bridge that spanned China Channel, Chew Lim met him.

"Get in," Lee said. "Which way?"

"To the northwest, about two miles from here along the levee road."

"Did you know the dead man?"

"I knew him well. His name is Lai Gulam. He and Sardar Lan have ruled my master's Hindu crews for ten years."

"Why do you think Sang Hop had him killed?"

"Because this dead Lai Gulam and his mate, Sardar Lan, have opposed Sang Hop for many years."

"Why was the dead man so far from his camp?"

"I cannot say. He may have visited the Seaborn Heaven to rescue some of his countrymen from Sang Hop's hands. Many of these India men smoke opium."

"You have used opium there?"

"At various times," Chew Lim confessed.

"Last night?"

"Aye, five or six pipes."

"The color?"

"Not black—red and rotten with dust that choked me with its smoke."

"A man creates his own hell," James Lee observed.

At the scene of the murder James Lee devoted ten minutes to his examination of the dead man. Then, absorbed in a complex series of problems that had developed with his discoveries of various elements of evidence, he turned and made his way up the sloping face of the embankment, inspecting every foot of the ground. Ending where Lai Gulam lay, the track of the dragged corpse was plainly visible. Where this track left the roadway on top of the levee James Lee halted. Directly before him in the motor road an oil-blackened area of dirt half as large as a man's hand claimed his attention. "The car stopped there." Four feet south of the oiled spot the ground was marked with a small crater formed by the impact of rust-stained water that had fallen from the leaking radiator. Near this lay the crushed body of a butterfly. Still attached to this, their orange and yellow markings brilliant against the brown earth, were two of the insect's wings. Four feet from the butterfly, toward the water side of the levee, James Lee found the stub of a brown-paper cigarette.

He picked this up and lighted it, inhaling two mouthfuls of the smoke. He threw the burning stub of the cigarette away and walked toward his car. To Chew Lim, abruptly, "Where is the companion of the dead Lai Gulam—the other foreman of the Hindu laborers, Sardar Lan?"

"He is probably working in the sugar beets along the north boundary of my master's land, six miles ahead."

James Lee started the car. He opened up to a perilous sixty.

Beyond the turn the rough roadway eastward along Fish River slowed their progress for two miles, and then, "There are the Hindu laborers," Chew Lim announced, lifting a trembling hand toward the broad field to the right. "The man with the stick—the bearded man with the black turban—that is Sardar Lan."

The siren on James Lee's car howled a brief note. Sardar Lan looked at the car for a moment and started across the field toward it.

"What you want?" he asked when he came up.

"Lai Gulam is dead," James Lee said.

Sardar Lan's eyes grew terrified.

"Who would kill Lai Gulam—with this?" From the pocket of his coat James Lee hauled out a six-foot length of brown, bloodstained cord. "See, the strangler's knot! Who hated Lai Gulam? Hindu man? India man? Sikh, not pray Mohammed like you? Maybe pray to Siva. Maybe Vishnu. Maybe..."

Interrupting, "I know what better do," Sardar Lan suggested. "You see Hindu priest of Siva temple. You ask him."

"Get into the car."

Racing back along the route toward Denman Hale's house, Chew Lim cast a questioning look at James Lee as they passed the Seaborn Heaven in Jordan Slough. "You are not attempting the capture of Sang Hop?"

"Not now."

"But he killed Lai Gulam and my master may be his prisoner—tortured—at this moment."

"That may be. I think not."

Denman Hale at the moment lay face down on the dank earth floor of the Siva temple. He alternated now through varying periods of consciousness. After a more complete returning to life he became vaguely aware of a subdued, droning chant, intoned by a robed figure in a thronelike chair. The chant ended and the recital of some ritual of devotion began. Hale filled his lungs with air that seemed to burn his swollen throat. He tried with his tongue to eject the cotton rag that filled his mouth. Failing, he whined in impotent rage.

The voice of the clacking priest was silent. Two turbaned men picked Hale up. They carried him to a narrow six-foot pit that they had dug in the earth floor and lowered him into it, feet first. His flexed legs could not support him and he slumped down until his head was a foot below the surface of the floor.

The priest of Siva resumed his chanting, voicing his devotion in hypnotic monotones barely audible to the half-conscious victim in the earthen pit.

After a little while Hale felt a cascading stream of rice grains falling upon his bowed head....

On the smooth highway, speeding toward Stockton at eighty miles an hour James Lee questioned Sardar Lan. "The Siva temple—who will be there now? What priests?"

"There will be Lakman Singh very sure. Always him. Also maybe strong man priest name Gadar."

"And Basanty Lai?"

Sardar Lan's eyes widened with astonishment. "You know before these bad men?"

"No, but I have ears." James Lee passed a loaded .38 revolver to Sardar Lan. "Which way now to the temple of Siva?"

"Five streets more," Sardar Lan said.

Half a block from his objective James Lee stopped the car. Old Chew Lim got out with Lee. "I go with you," he said.

"You would better remain here."

"I go with you," Chew Lim repeated in Cantonese. "Three are better than two if there is conflict."

"Come ahead."

Sardar Lan was fifty feet in advance. He turned in through the gate of a dilapidated frame house thirty feet back from the sidewalk. At the gate James Lee heard Sardar speak in Hindustani to someone inside the house. "Follow quickly," Lee said to old Chew Lim. "Sardar speaks to one of the men we seek."

In ten steps, with Chew Lim behind him, Lee was at Sardar's side. "They say not open door," Sardar whispered.

"Gadar Singh? Basanty Lai?"

Sardar nodded. "Yes. Both man."

Without a moment's hesitation James Lee pulled a .45 automatic from its holster under his left armpit and fired a shot through the lock on the door. "Now!" he said to Sardar. "Kick it in! Break it down!"

Sardar lunged at the door. It gave way with the second impact of his shoulder. James Lee walked over it into a long hallway that ran the full length of the house. There were three doors opening from this hallway on the right, two on the left. "Break into those three rooms!" he said to Sardar Lan. "And be on your guard!"

The two rooms to the left were empty. As Sardar opened the door of the middle room James Lee turned to the one at the end of the hall.

"No man here," Sardar called.

At that moment from the rear of the house James Lee heard a man's voice raised in a howl of pain, and under it a continuous cackle of Cantonese. "Old Chew has something!" But now there was no time for Chew Lim's affair, for from the opening door of the last room a blast of gunfire greeted James Lee. He felt the splintering panels of the door hitting against his chest, and the heavy air was suddenly acrid with the fumes of black powder. He dodged to the left, firing low at the shrouded figure of a man inside the room. There followed a groan of pain and a man's voice snarling invectives in guttural Hindustani.

On the instant Sardar Lan was at James Lee's side. "It is Basanty Lai," he said. "Let me go first."

Sardar dived through the door, his .38 ready for action, but Basanty Lai was out of the fight, writhing in pain on the dirt floor of the room. Sardar kicked his prostrate enemy. "Paying now with blood," he announced to James Lee. "He choke many other man dead without blood. Pay now with blood."

"Never mind that! Look! Quick!" In the half light of the room James Lee swung Sardar Lan around to face a seated figure, inert in a great chair, facing a gilded idol on a throne against the west wall of the room. "The priest of Siva! The goddess Kali is feasting on a victim the priest provides!"

"The priest is Lakman Singh," Sardar announced.

Between the gilded image of Siva and the inert priest, from a great brass bowl, suspended by three iron chains from an ebony tripod, a thin stream of rice grains fell, like the sand in an hourglass, into a circular pit in the dirt floor of the room. Seeing this, Sardar's eyes widened in horror. "The feast of Kali!"

He leaped to the rice-filled pit in the earthen floor and buried his hands in the cone of rice that had fallen from the brass bowl.

In three seconds, scooping out the rice with his cupped hands, "My master!" Sardar exclaimed.

James Lee with a glance at the inert figure of the priest, fell to the aid of Sardar Lan. A moment's work revealed Denman Hale's head. "He is net dead," James Lee announced. "He is breathing."

When the pair could reach Hale's armpits they hauled him upward.

"This man was twice near death," James Lee said to Sardar Lan. "Bring some cold water now. He is returning to life. And ask Chew Lim to..."

The siren of a patrol interrupted him. A moment later four police officers came into the room. "What's the shooting?" the first one asked. "What's going on in here?"

"I'm responsible," James Lee answered. "This is a federal job. My name is Lee. That man on the floor, and that opium sleeper in the chair—you can hold them for murder. Lend a hand here with this man, will you? He's Denman Hale—the Siva crew almost got him. One of you men telephone the sheriff to round up Sang Hop and his gang on the ark boat."

When two of the police officers had taken over the task of reviving Denman Hale, James Lee made a quick search for old Chew Lim. He found him on guard over the inert form of Gadar Singh. There was a noose of clothesline around Gadar's neck. "Mebbe choke him too much plenty allee same fashion him killum eprybody," Chew Lim explained in a loud voice, hoping the world might hear. In Cantonese, to James Lee, his voice trembling in anticipation of disaster, "My master—he met death?"

"He lives!" James Lee answered. "He had not quite finished the Feast of Kali that the Siva men prepared for him."

An hour later, to Denman Hale, “I had to guess fast,” James Lee confessed. “We knew that a lot of Indian opium was coming in. Old Chew Lim said Sang Hop's opium was red and dirty with dust. That's India stuff.... The cord that killed Lai Gulam—the lay of the strands, the long red fibers, the strangler's knot—obviously of India, probably a Siva-worshiping gang of thugs. The cigarette, typically Agra Chumbul leaf. Then the dead butterfly that had dropped from the radiator of Basanty Lai's car. The Indian opium has been coming into California from Nevada towns east of the Sierra. The butterfly was a mountain swallowtail—*Papilio indra*, and an imported stranger in this Delta country. Various other leads—but why bore you? Mostly guesswork. Ounce of brains and a ton of luck, that's the secret.”

Denman Hale rubbed a gentle finger over the livid scars on his neck. “Luck be damned!” he said. “I needed more than luck when you stormed in. I ran plumb out of luck late last night. A ton of brains! I'll tell the world. Boy, here's to you!”

JAYBIRD'S CHANCE

"I wouldn't bother you with this case, Mr. Lee," Melvin Armstrong explained, "except for the fact that the man who stole the gold is a Chinese—a countryman of yours. The sheriff's men can't make him talk. We've got the goods on him, all right, but he won't open up."

"What's the man's name?"

"His name is Wong Low."

James Lee nodded. "Probably a distant cousin of mine."

"I thought your name was Lee."

"My family name is Wong. Any Wong is my cousin."

Melvin Armstrong, president of the Gold Rock Mining Corporation, took time out to smile. "Forty million Chinese can't be Weng. Sorry. The point is this man Wong Low, who has been cook at the Payboy for the last six years, got away with two of our gold shipments. They don't amount to much but I want to find the gold."

"How do you know Wong Low is the thief?"

"His fingerprints were on the knob of the safe in the mine office, for one thing. The Bank of Canton issued a draft to his order for ten thousand in gold five days after the first brick was stolen. We discovered that yesterday and arrested him."

"Where are you holding him?"

"The sheriff has him in jail at Colburn."

"How far is the Payboy Mine from Colburn?"

"You turn off the main highway fifteen miles toward Paradise from Colburn—then it's three miles to Mad Creek and another three miles to where the road branches to the right. That's twenty-one miles. The branch road is about eight miles long. It runs down Mad Creek Canyon. That makes twenty-nine or thirty miles from Colburn. You can get out of the mine to the north, to Silica, over a stretch of mountain road. Twelve or fourteen miles. It isn't very feasible for a car. I wouldn't try it if I were you.... Will you look the job over for me?"

James Lee nodded. "I'll be very glad to. What were the gold shipments worth?"

"The first brick weighed slightly over eleven thousand dollars. The second one ran a little stronger—close to twelve thousand. I'm mighty glad you're on the job for us. I'll write a letter to Gorman. He's our superintendent at the Payboy." Melvin Armstrong pressed a button on his desk. "When can you get on the job?"

"I'll start for Colburn tonight," James Lee said. After a moment, "How do you usually make these gold shipments from the mine?"

"Good old Uncle Sam. Rural delivery carrier." "Who carried them from the mine to the Silica-Redhill Road?"

"The mail carrier goes up to the mine once a week. We aren't interested in him. The two bricks were stolen from the safe in the mine office. The first one three weeks ago and the second one day before yesterday. Just a moment and I'll dictate a note to Sam Gorman. You'll find Sam a good egg. If you like fishing, there are a lot of hungry trout in Mad Creek. Excuse me a moment."

To his secretary, "Take a letter to Gorman," Mr. Armstrong directed.

"Mr. Sam Gorman Superintendent, Payboy Mine

"Dear Mr. Gorman: This will introduce our confidential operative, Mr. James Lee. We feel sure that you will show him every courtesy and give him whatever assistance he requires.

"Melvin Armstrong."

"Bring that in here right away."

Turning to James Lee: "I understand that Gorman and some of the bays in the office play a pretty stiff game of poker up there at the mine. The best trout fishing in the world and a table stake game at night—I wish I could go along with you, Mr. Lee.... Or do you play poker?"

James Lee smiled. "I enjoy the game very much," he said.

The president of the Gold Rock Mining Corporation signed the letter to his superintendent when the secretary brought it in. He handed the letter to James Lee. "Good luck, Mr. Lee."

James Lee nodded. "I'll report progress when, as and if it develops. Good morning, Mr. Armstrong."

In Colburn, the county seat of Mountain County, after presenting his credentials to Sheriff George Dutton: "Mr. Armstrong tells me that you have an airtight case against Wong Low," James Lee said.

Sheriff Dutton nodded vehemently. "We've got that old sinner sewed up tighter than the horsehide cover on a baseball. Only thing that worries me is finding out what he done with that other gold brick."

Curtly, "What's the evidence against him?" Lee asked.

"In the first place nobody never seen no China boy get rich overnight unless he was gambling or stealing something or sold a woman," Sheriff Dutton began. "Five days after the Payboy's first gold shipment was stole Wong Low blossoms out with a bank draft for ten thousand dollars in gold. In the second place, one of my boys went up there and dusted the knob of the combination on the safe and found that Chinaman's thumbprints in three places on it. In the third place, he's a mighty slick individual. Every fan-tan game from Dutch Flat to Little York in the early days was busted sooner or later when he hit camp.

"He's been mighty slick and he got away with it. But now we got him. All that worries me is gettin' the gold back for Mr. Armstrong. I reckon that's where you step in. We been working him over with a short piece of rubber hose but he won't talk worth a cent." Sheriff Dutton's eyes glinted up suddenly, to meet James Lee's calm gaze. "You savvy his lingo?"

"I speak Chinese," James Lee said. "I would like to talk to Wong Low."

"Come along and I'll turn you loose with him in his cell. He's battered up some but he can still talk if he has to."

Facing his countryman when Sheriff Dutton had left them alone in Wong Low's cell in the county jail, "An ape may sit on a throne," James Lee said in Cantonese, nodding toward the departing sheriff. "Courage! A stone lion does not fear the rain."

Old Wong Low nodded his bandaged head. “Aye, an intelligent man recognizes the will of heaven.”

“Time is an arrow. Tell me your story quickly.”

Seated on his cot in the jail cell old Wong Low looked up at James Lee.

“The eyebrows of youth cannot compare with the beard of age,” he suggested. “The horseman does not know the footman's trials. I have stolen nothing.”

“You are an ant on a hot rock. Minnows can laugh at a stranded whale.”

“True enough,” Wong Low agreed. “Let me remind you, though, that the weight of a man's tongue can crush a giant.”

“A hunting dog does not feel his fleas. On the jail gates in the Central Glory are four words: 'You repent too late.'”

“I have nothing to repent. The tree for shade, the man for reputation. I have stolen nothing.”

“Where did you get the money to pay for the ten-thousand-dollar draft that the Bank of Canton issued to you?” James Lee asked.

“Through the labor of twenty years, I had entrusted my savings to various merchants of the Four Families in San Francisco. I had intended returning to the Central Glory this month—to rest. I have worked hard through long years in the gold hills.”

“Why were the prints of your fingers on the lock of the safe in the mine office?”

“The number two governor of the mine told me to make sure each night that the safe was locked.”

“You mean the engineer, young Mr. Darrell?”

Wong Low nodded. “That is his name,” he said.

“In the river of life no man can swim upstream,” James Lee suggested. “There is a last step to every journey.”

Wong Low bowed his head. “One moment of life can hold a thousand years of sorrow,” he said. “This jailer who keeps me captive, ren mien sheo hsin—the face of a man, the heart of a beast.”

“In this world of darkness heaven disposes,” James Lee suggested. “Have patience. Calamity can be changed into a blessing. *Ch'uh liao si ti.* You will emerge from this place of death. Only the blind see ghosts.”

"Maybe thou hast clear perception," Wong Low growled. "Who am I to question the will of heaven? I desire to regain the lost harmony of life—sweet after bitter. *Chiu peu-fen*—I have done my duty."

"Be silent," James Lee ordered suddenly. "Your jailer returns. Beside the tiger's mouth is a place of danger. Walk the middle path, practice right conduct. All will be well."

Looking directly at Sheriff Dutton, who had suddenly appeared at the door of Wong Low's cell: "I have just reminded Wong Low of one of our ancient proverbs—'It is always the smartest monkey that falls from the highest tree.'"

"Has he told you yet where he hid that second brick?" the sheriff asked. "We can get a court order for that gold draft. It's where he hid the second brick that worries me."

"Making these old men confess is a difficult problem," James Lee suggested. "Take it easy with him. I wouldn't beat him up any more if I were you. His lamp of life burns low—they die easily at his age."

"Whatever you say," Sheriff Dutton agreed. "What's your next move?"

"I'm going up to the Payboy Mine and have a look at the scene of the theft," James Lee answered. "Will you come up with me?"

"I'll be up in a day or two," the sheriff answered. "I can't get away right now. Both my deputies is down with the flu."

At Redhill, fifteen miles from Colburn, James Lee swung his car to the northwest along the Redhill-Silica road. Three miles away from the main highway he crossed Mad Creek on a new concrete bridge and entered the three-mile stretch uphill to the point where the narrow branch road led west-wardly to the Payboy Mine.

Along this road that paralleled Mad Creek he met no traffic. Part of the road was rough, but there were stretches through pine forest where the going was good, and here, careless of his driving, he gave himself over to a pleasurable contemplation of the beauties of the rugged country. Below him, visible through barren areas that broke the wooded slopes, Mad Creek, tumbling to the west, seemed to lie ready to confirm Melvin Armstrong's promise of good trout fishing. The mountain air was heavy with the scent of the pine woods, sweet with the smell of the tarweed that grew in the open glades. Through a sunlit corridor, deep in the pines, he saw three deer walking slowly up the gentle slope that lay back from the steep north bank of Mad Creek. "Good country," the traveler reflected. "Holiday country. I may prolong my stay."

It was nearly four o'clock when he got to the Payboy Mine. The sun lay behind a high mountain to the west and the air was suddenly chill. He drove past a bunkhouse, a cookhouse and a shaded bungalow. In front of the office of the Payboy he stopped his car. He entered the office and faced Sam Gorman. "I am James Lee," he said. "Here is a note for you from Melvin Armstrong. You are Mr. Gorman?"

"I'm what's left of him. I'm mighty glad to see you, Mr. Lee." A hearty handclasp and a warm smile on Sam Gorman's homely countenance left no doubt as to the sincerity of the superintendent's welcome. "Shake hands with Walter Darrell," Gorman invited. "That's him settin' at the drafting table. He's the engineer of this Payboy job. That's Tommy Miller settin' there at the desk. He's timekeeper and commissary boss and anything else that's got to be done. All of us feel like damn fools, workin' our heads off to drag a little gold out of the mountains and then having that doggone Wong Low get away with it. By rights I ought to have hung that Chinaman before the sheriff got him."

James Lee smiled. "You're perfectly sure that he's the thief?"

"They ain't nothin' to it," Sam Gorman answered. "Nobody had to git that fingerprint feller to prove it to me. I was sure it was him the minute Darrell told me the first brick was missing. We found his fingerprints on the knob of that safe over there and I was twice as sure. When the sheriff found out that the slant-eyed slicker had hid away ten thousand bucks in a bank draft on a Chinese bank I was so all-fired sure Wong Low was the thief that I come dern' near blastin' him into whatever Chinese hell he's headed for. I'd 'a' done it, only I was scared we'd never git no track of the second brick he stole. You have a talk with him down at Colburn?"

Lee nodded. "I talked with him for a while."

"You get a confession out of him?"

"Not yet. He's a hard man to handle."

"He's a mighty slick hombre. I suppose you'll want to dig into things right now. I've always wondered how a detective started to work on a case like this."

James Lee looked steadily at Sam Gorman. "I'm in no hurry to begin work. Tell me, are there any trout in the local stretch of Mad Creek? Do you suppose I could catch enough for supper if I'd go down there now?"

"Boy, you could get enough trout in one hour to feed all four of us. Ill lend you a fishing rig if you want it," Gorman offered.

"I think I'll fish for an hour. I haven't had any good trout fishing for five years."

"You catch a mess and bring 'em up here and that Greek flunky that took Wong Low's place in the kitchen will fry 'em to a fare-ye-well. You like to play poker?"

"I enjoy poker very much."

"We're doggone glad you come—win, lose or draw. Tommy Miller and Walter and me play three-handed nearly every night. Three-handed games ain't no good. Now and then Jim Saunders drifts in. That helps us out."

"Who is Jim Saunders?"

"He's a mighty good poker player. Deputy game warden in this district. Raises hell with the city folks that come up here after trout without no licenses. Dances with the gals down at Colburn doggone near every night and puts in the rest of his time plantin' these streams around here with trout. Jim Saunders is a mighty busy man. He's due through here the next day or two. We can have a five-handed game the night he shows up if he stays over....

"Come along and I'll lend you some old clothes if you ain't got none with you. You've got to wade Mad Creek to do any good with the trout."

At half past six, returning to the Payboy Mine with thirty trout to show for an hour's fishing, James Lee found a light truck standing in front of the mine office. In the body of the truck, insulated against the changing temperatures of the mountain air, sat twelve large milk cans. "Somebody from the trout hatchery planting more fish," James Lee surmised. "Jim Saunders, probably."

Greeting Sam Gorman, "The fish didn't hear that I was coming," the fisherman boasted. "I caught thirty beauties in two short stretches of water."

Sam Gorman chuckled. "Boy, you're mighty close to gittin' overtook with the law. You got a fishing license?"

James Lee smiled. "Guilty," he said. "Game warden driving that fish truck?"

"It's Jim Saunders. I guess maybe I can keep you out of jail this time. Come on in and meet Jim. We can have a five-handed game tonight."

The five-handed poker game opened up at eight o'clock, no limit and table stakes.

Half the hands played were draw poker with an occasional jack pot, but under the liberty of dealer's choice two of the players, Jim Saunders and young Walter Darrell, persistently elected to deal stud poker. "That's what the doggone war did to these birds," Sam Gorman complained, scowling at Jim Saunders after he had followed an ace in the hole to defeat in the face of three deuces. "Deal the cards."

Dealing the cards, "Play what you get. A hand of draw," Tommy Miller announced.

Under the gun James Lee picked up his hand. "I pass," he said blandly, mildly pleased at the sight of a pat straight running to the nine of diamonds.

"Ten bucks." Jim Saunders dropped two blue chips on the table.

"And fifty before the draw." Walter Darrell tipped over a neat pile of ten blue chips.

"I'll have a look." Sam Gorman met the bet.

"This is an interesting hand," James Lee commented. "All right, I suppose, if I draw to an ace?" He pushed twelve blue chips into the pile on the center of the table.

"That'll be fair enough," Walter Darrell said, "but you won't catch many more. I'm holding four of 'em pat right this minute.... Deal the cards."

Sam Gorman took one card.

"I'll play these," Jim Saunders announced.

James Lee lighted a cigarette. After a moment he tossed his pat straight into the center of the table face down. "Too rich for my blood. I'll bid my sixty bucks goodbye right now and sit on the side lines."

When the smoke cleared away Jim Saunders had captured a six-hundred-dollar pot with a colorful full house made up of queens and jacks.

"This is poker for blood," James Lee reflected. "I wonder how it is that these middle-weight-salary lads can mix in with such big money. I'll have to play 'em mighty close to keep from losing my shirt, but I've got to stay in the game."

Playing until midnight, nosing out with a fifty-dollar profit, James Lee was enabled to learn a number of things about his companions. Walter Darrell seemed to be reckless with money. Jim Saunders was careless with small bets, sure of himself with the larger ones. Sam Gorman was mildly drunk by eleven o'clock and lost a thousand dollars between then and midnight. Tommy Miller stayed out of the big pots. Gorman borrowed chips from Jim Saunders and forgot to pay them back.

At midnight Jim Saunders proposed another thirty minutes of play. He laid his watch on the table in front of him. It was a thin and beautiful watch made by Valentine of Geneva.

"That's a mighty nice watch," James Lee commented.

"Right," Jim Saunders returned. "She cost me four hundred bucks. Bought her last week in Reno from a New York man that went busted in a gambling joint. He said it cost him a thousand bucks."

James Lee nodded. "I don't doubt it a bit. That's a fine watch...."

An hour after midnight, after Jim Saunders had been parked away in a spare room in the bungalow and when Tommy Miller and Walter Darrell had retired to their rooms: "Let's have a drink," Sam Gorman invited James Lee.

After a long moment's careful survey of the glass of whisky that he held in his right hand, "There might be something in what this Chink says about being innocent," Sam Gorman began. "Did you see the way Darrell played his cards tonight?"

"He made some heavy bets for a salaried man."

"That's what I mean," Sam Gorman said. "I didn't tell you this, but it was natural enough for Wong Low's fingerprints to be on the knob of the safe. I heard Darrell tell him one time to see that it was closed every night. Darrell told him to see that the safe door was closed and to twist the combination."

"What is Darrell's record?"

"He's a Stanford man. He was in Denver for a while—he's been here three years," Sam Gorman answered. "His record is clear enough but he's notorious for pulling off a wild night two or three times a year in San Francisco. He bought a thousand dollars' worth of champagne at the Palace one night a year ago."

"I'll have a look at Darrell," James Lee said. "How about some sleep?"

"Fair enough. I'm going underground at seven o'clock. Would you like to come along?"

Smiling, James Lee shook his head. "Many thanks. I think I'll hit the trout again at sunrise. What time will you be back into daylight?"

"I'll see you at noon," Sam Gorman answered.

At sunrise three miles east of the Payboy on the mountain road that led to the Redhill-Silica highway, James Lee turned to his right and headed down the wooded slope that led to Mad Creek. The stream lay a thousand feet south of him at an elevation five or six hundred feet below the road.

Leaving the road for a little distance, he walked through a pine forest and then beyond a glade bright with the first blush of the morning sunlight he came to a thicket of ash and maple carpeted with a fragrant growth of tarweed. A congress of chattering bluejays attracted his attention. The blue-jay jamboree was being staged in the lower branches of a mountain laurel. Observing this, "Natural history be damned is their motto," James Lee reflected. "No bluejay ever played around a bay tree before.... I'll have a look-see at this."

Fifty feet from the mountain laurel he halted abruptly to watch with eager interest the retreat of a scurrying otter. "That's the first time I ever saw one of those animals so far from water in the daylight," James Lee reflected. "I wonder what he's doing up here."

Under the laurel tree, after the protesting cries of the blue-jays had silenced, James Lee found the lure that had attracted them; the pungent bait that had brought the otter out of his Mad Creek home. Over an area of five feet in diameter the browning carpet of leaves under the laurel tree was spotted with the glint of little fish. “Minnows—baby trout,” James Lee decided. Six feet to the left of the bluejays' banquet table, under a covering of decaying leaves that lay dark and wet against the lighter colors, James Lee found a canvas coin sack. Stenciled on the stained fabric in black paint he read the word “Payboy.” A piece of four-strand cotton cord lay ten feet away. He picked up the cord. Parts of it were stained black. “We win again,” he said, half aloud.

At eleven o'clock, to Walter Darrell in the Payboy office, “When Mr. Gorman comes into daylight tell him I've gone down to Colburn,” he said.

Young Darrell nodded. “Fair enough. Hurry back. We'll play four-handed tonight and I'll add a thousand dollars to my bank account.”

In Colburn, investigating Walter Darrell's bank account as his first bit of work in line of duty, James Lee spent ten minutes at the Colburn National Bank. Leaving there, he went direct to the offices of Sheriff Dutton in the county courthouse.

Greeting the sheriff after a moment, “I have a lead or two on this Payboy case,” James Lee said. “Will you help me out on it?”

“I'll do anything you say,” Sheriff Dutton announced heartily. “Melvin Armstrong just called me on long-distance. He told me to get word to you that Walter Darrell dropped two thousand dollars in a poker game at Jim Thome's place in San Francisco a month ago.”

“I'll look him over tonight,” James Lee said. “In the meantime hit this other detail with both feet. Arrest Jim Saunders. You'd better step on it. I've a hunch this case breaks wide open tomorrow.”

“I have a hunch you're haywire as hell,” the sheriff objected. “Never mind, it's your funeral. I'm taking orders. What time are you going to be down here tomorrow?”

“I'll be down before noon.”

“You're bringing Darrell with you, of course.”

James Lee's mouth hardened. “I'll bring him in,” he said.

An hour after midnight, when the four-handed poker game had ended, in seeming confidence to Sam Gorman, "I'm taking Walter Darrell down to Colburn tomorrow morning," Lee announced. "I want you to come along."

Sam Gorman's eyes widened in astonishment. "Have you got him cinched?"

"Not quite, but I think I can break him down. I don't want to make any false moves. The first thing we do is get him into the sheriff's office."

"I'll go with you. When do we start?"

"At ten o'clock tomorrow. Can you frame up some phony reason why you want him to go with us?"

"Plenty of 'em," Sam Gorman agreed.

At ten o'clock on the following day, carrying his suitcase, Sam Gorman stepped into James Lee's car with Walter Darrell. "I'm going on down to San Francisco for a couple of days," he explained, pointing to his suitcase. "I haven't had a day off for two months."

"All work and no play...." James Lee quoted.

In Sheriff Dutton's office with Sam Gorman and Walter Darrell after greetings had been exchanged, significantly, "Did you see Jim Saunders?" James Lee asked.

Sheriff Dutton nodded vehemently.

"Get a confession out of him?"

"Complete. Got one of the bricks and a mint certificate for the other one."

James Lee nodded toward Sam Gorman. Then to the sheriff, "Book the next man," he said.

Sam Gorman's mouth hardened. "You damned lousy Chink," he snarled, reaching back for a gun, "I'll blast you from here to Oregon!"

"Steady!" James Lee said quietly. A black automatic in his right hand punched suddenly into Gorman's stomach. "You're through. Next time when you tie up a gold sack don't use a piece of iodine-stained curtain cord out of your own bedroom. Next time when you park a gold brick in a can of fish you'd better tell your right bower not to dump the fish under a laurel tree. Bluejays don't like laurel trees."

"What are you talking about?"

James Lee scowled at the superintendent of the Payboy Mine. "I'm talking about the curtain cord in your bedroom and a convention of wild life that I found on Mad Creek," James Lee said quietly. "All the bluejays on earth had rallied round a little mess of trout that Saunders emptied out of one of his fish cans. I'm talking about that four-stranded curtain cord in the west window of your bedroom. Iodine on it. Iodine on the piece I found in the woods. Tough luck, big boy. You can try it again twenty years from now when you get out."

After reporting to Melvin Armstrong in San Francisco, "Thanks for the compliments," James Lee demurred, interrupting Armstrong's outburst of enthusiastic admiration. "I don't deserve them. Darrell's bank balance was fairly large. But his deposits, since the robbery, had been normal ones. That didn't clear him, of course. It looks as though luck did. Mostly luck—luck with the trout fishing, luck at the poker game and my happening to remember the stained curtain cord in Gorman's room when I dug up the Payboy coin sack that had held the second brick.... Old Wong Low reminded me of one of our ancient proverbs when the sheriff turned him loose. 'The eyes of the blind need no ointment.' Sometimes it isn't so much what you see as how you look at it."

NO WITNESSES

On a flying visit to San Francisco, the chief took time out to compliment James Lee on the capture of the Palmer narcotic crew.

"We are all proud of you," the chief said. "You had a close call when Palmer opened up on you with his gun."

James Lee smiled. "Three shots at ten feet. Two of them tore the lining out of my coat under the left arm."

"Your luck is still holding. May I have a cigarette?"

James Lee extended a package of cigarettes. The chief noted a faint tremor in the hand that held the cigarettes. "You need a holiday," he said. "Let Franklin take care of the office for a couple of weeks. Get out into the desert or the mountains."

"I don't need a holiday."

"Your nerves need a holiday. Orders are orders. Make your application for thirty days and I'll okay it."

In his smile of acceptance James Lee showed a quick eagerness for the rest from duty that his chief had given him. His mind turned forthwith to contemplation of the High Sierra. "I guess I will go up to Sky Ridge for a couple of weeks."

The chief nodded. "Fair enough; I wish I could go with you. After dinner, why don't you drive up? Only two hundred miles, isn't it?"

"That sounds pleasant. I'll be at Sky Ridge an hour after midnight."

On schedule, in the Ridge House at one o'clock in the morning, greeting Chester Greeley, the proprietor of the place, "I am here under cover," James Lee said. "I want a rest. If you don't mind we will avoid what happened last time when you introduced me as a Department man."

The affable Chester Greeley smiled. "Fair enough. I understand. No more bedtime stories for the trippers. No more request performances by the distinguished federal operative."

"Thank you. Is Old Hong Yet still with you?"

"He's still king of the kitchen. He will be glad to see you."

At breakfast next morning, to his Chinese friend, Hong Yet, who ruled the Ridge House kitchen, “I am here to eat, and to sleep, and to rest,” James Lee explained.

“I will be responsible for one of your three desires,” the old cook promised. “For your dinner tonight would you like six trout fresh from the icy water of Canyon Creek?”

“Twelve would please me even more.”

“Trust me. Your hunger will be satisfied.”

That evening at dinner the dining room of the Ridge House was filled, due to an influx of transient trippers bound for a midnight dance in a town fifty miles farther along the highway. When James Lee came into the dining room, the proprietor of the Ridge House introduced another guest. “I am sorry that we are so crowded tonight,” Chester Greeley explained. “This is Mr. Archer Long of Kansas City. If you gentlemen will share one of those small tables together, I will see that young Harper takes care of you right away.”

James Lee bowed. “Very happy to meet you, Mr. Long.”

“Mr. Long is going to be with us for a month,” Greeley explained. “He comes from Kansas City.”

Shaking hands with James Lee, “What business are you in, Mr. Lee?” Archer Long asked.

“I am interested in two or three enterprises in San Francisco,” James Lee said, veiling the truth with a plausible veneer of deceit.

“Business in Chinatown?”

Here the truth would serve. “Yes,” James Lee answered; “a lot of my business is in Chinatown.”

“I have a brass foundry in K. C,” Archer Long offered. “Started her on a shoestring twenty years ago and now she keeps me in expense money, at least. Haven't laid off a man in the last ten years.”

“You are very fortunate.”

Archer Long smiled. “I get the business—lots of railroad business. You been out here long?”

“I have lived in California most of my life.”

“This here country looks mighty good to me. The more I see of it the better I like it. I have a mighty good mind to settle down right here in the mountains and spend the rest of my days loafing and hunting and fishing.”

Within forty-eight hours after Archer Long's arrival in Sky Ridge, the spell of the California gold country had claimed him. To the loafing crew of old-timers on the front porch of Ed Hall's saloon, in the little mining town half a mile from the Ridge House, "Gentlemen, I'm stuck on this country," Mr. Long announced after he had enjoyed his second glass of beer. "I am going to buy me a place right here in this town and spend the rest of my days hunting and fishing and loafing around with you boys."

After a moment's silence, "They ain't no good places fer sale any more," Ed Hall declared. "Only land I know of close around here that you might get is the Levi Minch property. His father left him the place, you know. He's kind of sentimental and I don't know whether he will sell out or not."

"Levi don't need no money," one of the gang suggested.

"He likes money just the same," another member countered. "Levi has been a regular tightwad ever since he hit that rich placer ground near Little York."

Archer Long touched a match to a middle-class ten-cent cigar. "What would it take to buy the Minch place?" he asked.

Ed Hall munched on a chew of fine cut, and then, "I have seen the time when Levi would sell the whole twenty acres for five hundred dollars, but I tell you what to do, Mr. Long. You get ahold of two thousand dollars in small-size greenbacks. Go down and see Levi and slap the money down on the table in front of him and see what happens. It's worth trying."

"I'll take your advice; I'll try it. Right now I think I will amble up and have a look at the place."

Absorbed in contemplating the delights of a peaceful existence on the Levi Minch place, Mr. Long detoured to his left en route to the Ridge House, pacing slowly up the main street of Sky Ridge until he came to the Minch property. He stood a while looking out across the interesting terrain, noting with unrealized pleasure the play of light and shadows that painted and darkened the rocks and pines of his desired domain.

"She's perfect," he said half aloud, so that his own ears might share the happy mood that filled his heart. The mood endured through the long mile of his route to Ridge House, and at supper time, after speaking pleasantly to James Lee, who sat across the table from him, "It don't make any difference what you bring me for my supper," he said to young Gerald Harper. "Boy, this mountain air makes me so hungry I could eat the roast ribs of a cast-iron mule."

"I'll get you a nice, tender steak, Mr. Long. If old Hong Yet turns out a tough one I'll chase him over the bluff."

"I'll leave it to you, son," Mr. Long said with a royal gesture. "Anything goes, and the more the better. I'm hungry like a wolf."

When the waiter had left them, "That's a mighty fine boy, Mr. Lee," Archer Long declared. "He tells me he is working his way through college. I'll bet he makes a million dollars before he is through."

James Lee nodded. "No doubt," he agreed. "After all, nothing takes the place of hard work. He seems to be an excellent young man."

At the moment in the kitchen of the Ridge House the excellent young man faced old Hong Yet. "Cut loose with one of those nice tenderloin steaks for Mr. Long," he ordered. "Fry it in butter; he wants it rare."

"I ketchum. How much money he give you?"

"Listen, yau Oriental pirate, I'll split the dough with you when I get it. Hurry up with a good tender steak and all the trimmings."

James Lee had finished his dinner and had left the table before the tender steak was brought on. It tasted well, and Mr. Long complimented young Gerald Harper and old Hong Yet on their good work.

He handed the young man a silver dollar. "Son, buy yourself a house with this," he said.

"Thank you, Mr. Long."

Hungry for conversation, "You going to have money enough to take you through the next term?" Archer Long asked.

"Looks like I'm all set. I've got enough for my tuition and I can take on the battle of board and room when it comes along."

"You told me you was studying to be a mining engineer."

"Yes, sir. That's what I want to be."

"Get me a piece of pie and I'll make a proposition to you when you get back here."

Following the pie came Mr. Long's proposition: "Tomorrow morning right after breakfast I want you to drive me down to

Colburn. I want to get me some money at the bank. It'll take me about thirty seconds."

"Yes, sir; I'll have the car gassed and ready."

Archer Long's estimate of the time he would require in the Colburn bank was in error by more than seven minutes, but presently, with a thick bundle made up of one hundred twenty-dollar bills parked in his right hip pocket, he left the bank and returned to where young Gerald Harper waited for him in the car.

"I cleaned that up mighty quick," he said to Harper. "They dug up two thousand dollars for me in twenty-dollar bills without a struggle.... We might as well head back to Sky Ridge. I'm gittin' hungry for my lunch already."

Three hours after he had finished his lunch Archer Long left the Ridge House and walked to Ed Hall's saloon in Sky Ridge. Quietly, across the bar, after his second gulp of cold beer, "I'm going to walk down to Minch's place and play my ace like you advised," he confided to Ed Hall. "I went down to the bank this morning and got two thousand bucks in twenties. I'm going to slap 'em down in front of Minch and see what happens."

At nine o'clock, after serving coffee to the last supper guest in the dining room of the Ridge House, Gerald Harper walked back to the kitchen and faced old Hong Yet.

"Mr. Long hasn't showed up," he said. "Those trout that you're saving for him aren't going to get any better in the ice chest. How about cooking them for my supper?"

"You supper!" Hong Yet spluttered. "What name you! Boss he say keep fishee for Mis' Long. I keep him."

"Listen, you flathead. Mr. Long isn't going to fall for any antique fish. Go on and cook 'em and we'll split 'em fifty-fifty."

Old Hong Yet reached dramatically for a meat cleaver. "You talkee-talkee lilly bit more I split you fitty-fitty so big you die."

Falling back on the vernacular, scowling at his opponent, "Oh, yeah? You and who else?" Gerald Harper retorted. "Listen, you slant-eyed...."

Interrupting the battle at this point, Chester Greeley, proprietor of the Ridge House, appeared in the doorway of the kitchen. "What's going on here?"

"I was just trying to get Hong to cook those trout for me that he is saving for old man Long."

"Never mind about those trout. Save 'em for Mr. Long's breakfast. Didn't he show up for supper?"

"He hasn't showed up yet."

"Probably eating supper with some of his new friends over in Sky Ridge. Keep the trout for his breakfast."

Early the following morning the trout theme, lingering in Chester Greeley's mind, impelled him to inquire about Archer Long. "Mr. Long show up for his trout?" he asked, sampling the coffee that Gerald Harper had served.

"Not yet, Mr. Greeley."

"That's funny. Slip over to his cabin and see if he's asleep. He's always up before I am."

Three minutes later, returning from his inspection trip, "He isn't in his cabin," Gerald Harper reported. "He didn't sleep in his bed."

Chester Greeley frowned. "I wonder where he spent the night. That's the first time the old boy has stayed out all night."

In Sky Ridge, an hour later, Chester Greeley stopped at the post office and then made his way down to Ed Hall's saloon. "Morning, Ed," he said gravely, "how are you feeling?"

"Okay and then some. How's everything?"

"Fair enough.... You haven't seen anything of Mr. Long, have you?"

"He was here yesterday afternoon. That's the last I seen of him. Didn't he show up at your place?"

"He wasn't there for supper and he didn't sleep in his cabin last night. You don't suppose he was walking around and broke his leg or anything?"

"It ain't likely. All he had to do was yell loud and somebody would hear him."

"Well, I'll be going along. Ask the boys when they drift in if any of them know about Mr. Long."

"I'll look around," Ed Hall promised.

After he had swept out his establishment and sprinkled the rough floor Ed Hall turned his joint over to the first native that showed up and headed for Levi Minch's ranch.

Answering Ed Hall's first direct question, "Long come in here early yesterday evening," Levi Minch answered. "He stayed about half an hour."

"What did he talk about mostly?"

Levi Minch hesitated for a moment and then, "Well, mostly he talked about wantin' to buy this place. He was ready to pay cash."

Ed Hall grunted. "What made you think he could pay cash?"

Levi Minch's eyes glittered for a moment. "The main reason was that he had the cash with him—two thousand dollars."

Ed Hall, in feigned surprise, permitted a startled look to occupy his rugged countenance. "You mean that feller showed you two thousand dollars all in a bunch?"

Levi Minch nodded. "Yep. Two thousand dollars all in twenty-dollar bills."

"I always knowed you was crazy. You mean you let that much money get away when it was right in front of you?"

"Well, doggone it—I wanted time to think things over. I told him I'd let him know today."

When Ed Hall had returned to his haven he found six of the regular rest crew lounging on the front porch. "You fellers come in here," he said.

When the seven men were in the barroom, "Lock that front door," the proprietor ordered. Then point by point he set forth the reasons for his suspicion that Levi Minch might have murdered Archer Long. "That's the whole case in a nutshell," he concluded. "You know how Levi is about money."

"The only thing to do is to call up the sheriff. That's the best way. Tell him to come up here and look Levi over."

Ed Hall nodded, "I'll do it. I'll telephone Joe right now."

Searching Levi Minch's cabin, Joe Banfield, the sheriff of the county, and one of his skillful deputies found Archer Long's tobacco pouch and a leather coat that had belonged to the missing man.

"He gave me that pouch for a present," Levi protested.

"How about the leather coat?"

"He left it here because he was sweatin' and didn't want to carry it. He was comin' back for it."

"He didn't leave that pack of twenty-dollar bills in that coat, did he?" the sheriff asked abruptly.

"What twenty-dollar bills?" Levi Minch gulped.

"Levi, you know damn' well what twenty-dollar bills I mean. You seen 'em, didn't you?"

"I never saw...." Levi Minch began; then, remembering his statement to Ed Hall, "Yes, I saw the money," he said.

After a moment, "Levi, I got to take you with me," the sheriff said quietly.

Searching for Archer Long's body, half of the males of Sky Ridge and various guests and employees from the Ridge House spread out over the country lying around the Minch ranch.

Leading one of the searching parties, Chester Greeley, with young Gerald Harper, James Lee and four other guests from the inn, ranged southward from Levi Minch's cabin. Their search, fruitless up to that time, concentrated on a definite objective after a suggestion offered by young Gerald Harper.

"There's a prospect hole half a mile the other side of Minch's cabin—deep enough to hide a hundred murdered men," he said. "Let's try it."

Chester Greeley swung around. "Come on, men! That sounds mighty smart to me. Let's go."

Within the hour the crumpled body of Archer Long was found at the bottom of the forty-foot prospect hole half a mile north of Levi Minch's cabin. He had been killed with a blow back of his right ear that had fractured his skull.

"He might have fallen into the shaft," James Lee said. "I can't see much conclusive evidence of murder."

"If his skull was fractured falling down this shaft there'd be plenty of blood spilled around," Gerald Harper contradicted.

"That cinches the case against Minch," Chester Greeley exclaimed. "If it had been an accident he'd still have them twenty-dollar bills on him. A man don't rob himself falling down a prospect hole." Then to Young Harper, "Boy, one man's luck is another man's poison. If they convict Minch on what you figured out you got a thousand dollars coming to you—standing reward in this country for every convicted murderer."

"It's mighty sad money," Gerald Harper answered, "but I can use it. It'll pay my way through school."

At the Ridge House, returning with the sad news of Archer Long's death, Chester Greeley encountered his cook. "What you likee I do with Mis' Long fishee?" Hong Yet asked. "I keep him?"

"Eat 'em, throw 'em away, do anything you want with them! Mr. Long will never come back. He's dead. Somebody killed him."

"Too bad. Mis' Long number one good man. Who kill him?"

"Levi Minch killed him. He was over at Minch's place. Mr. Long had a lot of money on him. Next thing we find is his body. No money. Somebody robbed him."

Hong Yet grunted. "You talkee like you crazy. Levi Minchee him number one good man. He never kill eprybody."

"Stop talking to yourself." Chester Greeley started out of Hong Yet's kitchen. "Stop talking and get to work."

Hong Yet got to work, but for the ensuing hour for varying brief intervals he talked to himself in Cantonese.

Interrupting the soliloquy when it had dwindled to an occasional whispered phrase of criticism for Levi Minch's accusers, young Gerald Harper walked into the kitchen. "I want to use your big tub, China boy," he said. "All right with you?"

"Why you allee time likee big tub? Mo' better you ketchum lilly dishpan."

"I want to wash my corduroys. I'm going back to school next week and I got 'em gummed up with tarweed last week. How about it?"

"You likee big tub you take him."

"Okay, slant-eye."

For a little while after loaning his pet washtub, Hong Yet grumbled to himself at the indignity of lending this part of his personal equipment for laundry purposes and then, halting midway of a cackling sentence, he looked vacantly into space for five seconds. Forthwith, at a quick pace, he walked to his little room at the end of the kitchen. There he found two opium pills. He swallowed these and, his nerves steadying under the effect of the timely blessing, he sought his countryman, James Lee.

Following appropriate salutations, “My heart is heavy with a problem for whose solution I seek your aid,” he said. He continued for three minutes with fluent phrases, setting forth the problem. “The eyes of the blind need no ointment.”

“You are of clear perception,” James Lee said. “Wisdom adorns your words. I will see if we can solve this puzzle. Let me have the pieces of burned pages from the book.”

Twenty minutes later, in the narrow telephone booth of the pay station in Sky Ridge, James Lee took a charred fragment of paper out of his pocketbook. He called the State Library in Sacramento. Presently to one of the librarians, “My problem is this,” he said. “I have a scrap of a page from a burned book. I want to discover the name of the book. In the first line at the top of the page are the words: 'accumulated in cavities'. The rest of the fragment is rather obscure except two or three lines farther down in italics the text reads: 'Amalgam. See Page 130'. I want to identify that page. Probably a book on mineralogy. I'll telephone you again in an hour. I'm very anxious to discover the title of the book from which the burned page was taken.”

At five o'clock, following his second telephone call to the State Library, “I wonder if you can get young Gerald Harper rounded up for a brief and confidential conference,” James Lee said to Chester Greeley.

“You want to see him in line of duty?”

“Yes, if you can arrange it.”

“Go up to my bedroom. It's the second door to the left from the head of the stairs. I'll bring him right up. Do you want me to duck out and leave you together?”

“I very much want you to be present.”

“I'll stick.”

Facing Gerald Harper, “I'd like to get more of your theories about Archer Long's murder,” James Lee said. “You have covered all the country around the Levi Minch property, haven't you?”

“Most of it, Mr. Lee. Prospecting.”

“The Minch property wasn't included in one of the early Spanish grants, was it? Or do you know?”

"No, I don't know about the title. I don't think the Spanish grants came up into the gold country."

"Do you recall any mention of placer gold in the Spanish land grants in that book that James D. Dana wrote? What was it—Two Years Before the Mast?"

"That wasn't James D. Dana," Gerald Harper corrected. "He was a mineralogist. Two Years Before the Mast was written by another Dana. I think his name was Richard Henry Dana."

Very emphatically, "No, you're mistaken. James D. Dana wrote the book. I am sure of it," James Lee asserted.

"I'll bet you a million dollars you're wrong, Mr. Lee. I happen to know that James D. Dana is the author of several books on mineralogy. I'm studying that subject at school. I know what I'm talking about."

"Listen, boy, I've got seven or eight different editions of Two Years Before the Mast," James Lee explained. "I happen to know that book. I'll take your million-dollar bet. By any chance have you a copy of your Mr. James D. Dana's Mineralogy?"

"Of course, I..." At this Gerald Harped stopped.

"Go ahead. What were you going to say?"

"I was going to say that..."

"You were going to say that you had a copy of James D. Dana's Mineralogy. Is that it?"

Hesitating and then very slowly, "That's what makes me sure—I know the book perfectly well. I've studied it for three years. I've got a copy...."

"Where have you got a copy?" James Lee asked quietly.

"I've got a copy stored with my books down at school."

"What you've got at school proves nothing." Coldly then and abruptly, "By any chance would you have concealed one hundred twenty-dollar bills in your mutilated copy of Dana's Mineralogy?"

Gerald Harper's face crimsoned. He scowled at James Lee and then, in a voice that dripped with venom, "I can make trouble for you if you're not mighty careful, Mr. Lee. That accusation ..."

"Perhaps I have reason to accuse you," James Lee suggested. "The tarweed on your corduroys.... Why were you in such haste to borrow old Hong Yet's tub? Bloodstains, by any chance?"

Before Gerald Harper could answer, "The tarweed detail is interesting," James Lee continued. "Strangely enough, the only patch of tarweed within three miles of here lies in that area where we found Archer Long's body. Old Hong Yet smelled the odor of tarweed on your corduroys yesterday. The pungent aroma of tarweed disappears in twenty-four hours."

Gerald Harper scowled.

"What of it? That means nothing."

James Lee smiled thinly. "Why did you burn seventy or eighty pages of Dana's Mineralogy? Let me return to my original question. By any chance did you conceal Archer Long's money in your hollowed-out copy of that book after you killed him?"

In a moment, speaking slowly, "What if I have Mr. Long's money?" Gerald Harper grated. "It proves nothing. He might have given it to me. I didn't kill him."

James Lee nodded wearily. Then his eyes seemed to narrow to flaming points of green light. "How about a couple of witnesses?" he suggested. "What if two of the old-timers of Sky Ridge prospecting in the tarweed country near Minch's cabin watched you trailing Archer Long? What if they saw you kill him? Shall I bring them in?"

The young man's face turned gray. He took one deep breath. "I killed him," he admitted. "I didn't know anyone saw me do it."

James Lee lighted a cigarette. "No one saw you kill him," he said. "I merely suggested that there might have been witnesses." He turned to the proprietor of the Ridge House. "Please telephone the sheriff that we have Archer Long's murderer," he directed.

Again to Gerald Harper, "You made two mistakes," James Lee explained. "First of all, you overlooked Hong Yet's selfish interest in his pet washtub. Your second mistake was trying to burn the pages cut out of Dana's book in a trash fire. Trifling mistakes, I admit, but I am afraid you lose. I am sorry that you must pay with your life for having left the Middle Pathway. In China they say that a grain of sand can hide a mountain, and that only a dead snake is straight."

THREE WORDS

On the day before his expedition started west from Peiping, Alan Markham turned a collection of minor details over to Howard Lin, his Chinese assistant, and resigned himself to an afternoon's relaxation. The Chihli Plate was being run and a ten-dollar bet on a Mongol pony named Princess brought him a hundred silver dollars.

That night to Howard Lin, "We're starting lucky. I won at the races today," he said.

Lin smiled at his chief. "I hope we have the same luck west of the Little Gobi."

"We'll have plenty of luck," Markham predicted.

Against this prediction Old Man Trouble rode with the explorers for a thousand miles across the desert and then, beaten to a pulp, he was driven to retreat by the superior forces of Lady Luck.

Returning to the United States eighteen months after his departure from Peiping, Markham brought to Berkford University a treasure of ancient manuscripts and trophies in stone and metal that had been recovered from the haunted sands of the Takla Makan.

Howard Lin came back to the university with his chief to help Markham with some of the translations of the manuscript. A month after Markham had finished his preliminary report, and while he was still engaged with his first general classification of the earlier documents that had been found in a cliff south of the Tarim River, he was discovered dead in his residence.

To the coroner's jury, testifying relative to Alan Mark-ham's death, "I saw his hand sticking out of the window about ten minutes after four in the morning," Peter Barton said. "I only been working for the Jersey Dairy since November last year, but all the time since I begun delivering down the peninsula the professor took a quart a day. His hand was caught in the window screen and it was kind of bloody on the wrist. There was not much blood."

Q: What did you do when you saw the dead man's hand?

A: I was scared. I called out, "Hey, Professor!" and then I stood up and looked inside the bathroom. The light was burning. He was hanging down from his hand where it was caught in the screen window. I run to my truck and headed for the first telephone I thought of down at the Nite Bite Lunchery on the highway.

Q: To whom did you telephone?

A: First I got two nickels for a dime from the cook. And then I called up the police department.

Q: Not the sheriff of the county?

A: No, sir. I never give him a thought.

The records show that Sergeant Miller of the police department was informed of the discovery of Professor Markham's body at 4:16 a.m. Forthwith upon receipt of the information Sergeant Miller directed Peter Barton to return to Professor Markham's house.

Sergeant Miller then called Dr. Garner and, after informing him of the milkman's discovery, requested Dr. Garner to meet him at once at Professor Markham's house on the campus.

After he had completed his call to Dr. Garner, Sergeant Miller put another call through for Harvey Ainsworth, the comptroller of the university.

Sergeant Miller arrived at Professor Markham's house at 4:35 a.m., at which time he found the milkman, Pete Barton, and the comptroller of the university, Harvey Ainsworth, in the house.

Questioned by the coroner, Sergeant Miller testified in part as follows:

Q: Where was Professor Markham's body when you got to the house?

A: He was still hanging by his wrist from the screen window in his bathroom.

Q: You walked into the bathroom?

A: The first thing I done when I got to the professor's house after I seen Mr. Ainsworth and the milkman was to walk in and look at the dead man.

Q: How did you know he was dead?

A: Anybody could tell he was dead.

Q: Did you feel his pulse, listen to his heart?

A: There wasn't any need of that. Dr. Garner got there while the three of us was talking. The first thing he said after he spoke to Mr. Ainsworth, when he saw the body, was that the professor was dead.

Q: Of suicide or murder or death from natural causes, which did you instinctively decide upon? That is—I mean, did you have any ideas on this subject?

A: No, sir. The only thing I thought of was burglary. I kind of looked at the professor to see if he was shot or hit in the head with something or anything.

To Howard Lin, a Chinese: You were well acquainted with Professor Markham?

A: I have been studying with Professor Markham for two years.

Q: He employed you as an assistant?

A: Yes, sir.

Q: When did you last see Professor Markham alive?

A: I had supper with him on Friday evening. He told me we would have an early supper because he had a lot of work to do that night.

Q: What time did you last see him alive?

A: About nine o'clock that night.

Q: Mr. Lin, in the professor's bathroom did you see the bottle containing the poison that killed him?

A: Yes, sir. It was standing on the glass shelf above the wash bowl in the bathroom.

Q: Did you touch the bottle?

A: No, sir. It was none of my business. My chief was always taking some kind of medicine for his indigestion.

Following Howard Lin, Dr. Lyman Garner was sworn in by the coroner.

To Dr. Garner, "We can dispose of the formalities, Doctor," the coroner said. "Please tell us in plain language what you discovered at the time you found Professor Markham's, body."

A: The man was dead. Death was due to poison. The poison was hydrocyanic acid.

Q: Have you any theory as to how Professor Markham's wrist happened to be caught in the screen window of his bathroom?

A: Paralysis of respiration is one of the characteristics of a fatal dose of hydrocyanic acid. The symptoms are those of sudden and complete asphyxia. A full dose produces a sudden paralysis of the heart. A smaller amount, still fatal, might permit some volitional movements to be made before death. In my opinion, Professor Markham attempted in his last moments of life to open his bathroom window and fell dead at that moment. The odor of the hydrocyanic acid was unmistakable in the residue of contained air in the professor's lungs.

Q: Dr. Garner, would you say that the professor committed suicide?

A: I cannot say yes or no to that question. The broken tumbler on the bathroom floor had contained a solution of hydrocyanic acid. A small bottle containing a strong solution of hydrocyanic acid was on the glass shelf above the wash bowl in the bathroom.

Q: Did you record a description of the bottle and its label? ... Of course, Doctor, you understand we require your answer to the question merely for the record.

A: I understand. The bottle was a two-ounce bottle. The stopper was some composition substance covering a glass tube similar to an eye dropper with a rubber bulb at the end so that the dosage could be measured.

Q: Pardon me, Doctor, how much of the solution was in the bottle? Was it full?

A: Practically full.

Q: Was the stopper in the bottle when you saw it?

A: No, sir, it was lying on the glass shelf above the wash bowl.

Q: Do you recognize this bottle as being the one that contained the poison?

A: It looks like the same bottle.

Interruption by Sergeant Miller: “Excuse me. I made a record of the label on the bottle. It was Prescription No. 77,853 from Ehrmann's Pharmacy. Dr. Emmett prescribed it.”

The coroner nodded to Sergeant Miller. “Thank you,” he said.

“Dr. Emmett is up at Lake Tahoe on a vacation,” Sergeant Miller continued. “I telephoned him this morning. He said he never prescribed no poison for the professor.”

With mild impatience the chief inquisitor nodded again at Sergeant Miller. “Just a moment, Sergeant,” he suggested. “I have not finished with Dr. Garner.”

Then, resuming with Dr. Garner: Doctor, have you any theory as to why the deceased should have possessed a bottle of deadly poison?

A: The only thing that occurs to me is that in writing the prescription Dr. Emmett may have used an ambiguous contraction in Latin that might mean either hydrocyanic acid or hydrochloric acid. Hydrochloric acid may be useful in atonic dyspepsia and acidity of the stomach.

Q: And such an ambiguous contraction might result fatally to the patient?

A: Yes, indeed. A great many physicians in their ignorance of case endings in Latin grammar are apt to...

Interrupting Dr. Garner: “Thank you, Doctor,” the coroner said. “We will have Mr. Ehrmann sworn—and his pharmacist, Mr. Frank Ramsay.”

Presently to Ludwig Ehrmann: You are the proprietor of Ehrmann's Pharmacy?

A: Yes, sir.

Q: From your records, who compounded Prescription No. 77,853 dated on the label on this bottle 7-26-35?

A. My junior pharmacist, Mr. Frank Ramsay.

Q: Thank you, Mr. Ehrmann. That is all....

Q: Mr. Ramsay? Do you recognize the label on this bottle?

A: Yes, sir, I wrote the typewriting on it.

Q: I asked you to bring your file of prescriptions with you. Have you got the original prescription for the contents of this bottle, written by Dr. Emmett?

A: Yes, sir, I brought the file with me.

To his associates when the prescription of Ehrmann's Pharmacy had been presented in evidence, “Gentlemen, you see that this prescription is one of those 'ambiguous contractions of the Latin term' that Dr. Garner told us about. You will read in the first line of Dr. Emmett's prescription in his handwriting, 'Acid. Hydroc' Dr. Garner tells us that the term might mean either hydrochloric or hydrocyanic acid and that the first chemical in small doses might be harmless, while a few drops of the second chemical which killed Professor Markham would mean death. I regret to say that it becomes necessary to assume that young Mr. Frank Ramsay made an error in compounding the prescription."

At this, springing to his feet, "Mr. Ramsay made no error in compounding the prescription," Ludwig Ehrmann protested. "What sort of a fool would do a thing like that? You see on the label the prescription was dispensed by F.R. and checked by L.E.—that means me—'Ludwig Ehrmann.' We never make mistakes."

The coroner smiled thinly. "So you never make mistakes, Mr. Ehrmann.... There is always a first time. Maybe this is your first mistake."

"We have never made a mistake with a prescription," Mr. Ehrmann exploded. "In thirty-five years! We carry no cyanide in solution. It is in crystals."

The coroner nodded coldly. "Thank you, Mr. Ehrmann. Please be seated."

"*Gott im Himmel*!" Mr. Ehrmann exploded, glaring in anger at the coroner. "Yes! I will be seated." He resumed his chair heavily.

When Mr. Ehrmann was seated there was a moment's silence and then to the foreman of the jury, "It is reasonably evident that Professor Markham came to his death because of an error made in compounding a medicine prescribed by Dr. Emmett. It is a reasonable assumption that the pharmacist who filled the prescription, Mr. Frank Ramsay, is culpable. I request you to bring in a verdict of accidental death by hydrocyanic acid solution self-administered. I recommend that the pharmacist, Mr. Frank Ramsay, be held on a technical charge of manslaughter."

Turning to the young pharmacist, "This, of course, is highly unfortunate for you, Mr. Ramsay, but it seems to be the only course I can take in the matter.... There is, however, one more witness to testify—Ota Haruki."

"I am a student in the university," Haruki affirmed. "I have been attending Professor Markham's classes."

Q: You work for the professor?

A: Yes, sir. I cook supper for him three or four times a week.

Q: He had other servants?

A: No, sir.

Q: When did you last see him alive?

A: Friday evening about nine o'clock.

Q: Was the Chinese, Howard Lin, with him at the time?

A: No, sir. Lin left before nine.

Q: What about this bottle that contained the poison—did you see it?

A: Yes, sir. It was in the bathroom on the glass shelf above the wash bowl.

The coroner nodded at Haruki: "Thank you, that is all."

Three days after young Frank Ramsay, charged with manslaughter, was released on bail, Ota Haruki called at the office of the comptroller of Berkford University.

Facing the comptroller, "There was one matter relative to the death of Professor Alan Markham that was not brought out at the coroner's inquest," the Japanese stated. "I would like to ask your advice."

After the Japanese left the comptroller's office, Ainsworth put a call through to San Francisco for James Lee. "This Markham case, Mr. Lee," Ainsworth began. "I would like to talk to you about it. There is a new angle. Can I see you tonight?"

"Nine o'clock at my apartment in San Francisco—would that suit you?"

"Excellent, thank you. I will see you at nine o'clock."

That night, "This Markham affair has become definitely complicated by a new element," Ainsworth said to James Lee.

"One of Markham's students, a young Japanese who worked for him around the house, insists that Markham was murdered."

James Lee nodded.

"That is probable."

"You are familiar with the case?" Surprise lay in Ainsworth's voice.

"We have a transcript of the coroner's records in the department's local files. The Japanese is Ota Haruki?"

"Yes—Haruki. He outlined evidence that makes me feel almost sure that Markham was murdered."

"By whom?"

"By Howard Lin. Lin was helping Markham with the translations of the manuscripts that the expedition brought back. There is good reason, I think, to suspect that Lin is guilty of Markham's murder."

James Lee closed his eyes for a moment. "The motive?" he asked.

"Treasure! A million dollars—maybe five million dollars for the first man who finds it."

Smiling thinly, "Sailing directions complete from A to Z set forth at length in some old manuscript?"

"That's it exactly! The manuscript has disappeared from Markham's collection. Beside Markham, Howard Lin is the only man who had access to the lost document—that is, Lin is the only person who worked with Markham on classifying and translating the stuff.""How does Haruki know it was a treasure manuscript?"

"Haruki overheard Lin reading the preliminary translation of the document to Markham on the night of his death."

"Where did Markham keep these manuscripts?"

"In the vaults at the Memorial Library. He worked at his residence, where he had his own photographic equipment."

"This work that Markham did at his house—did he return the manuscripts he was investigating to the Memorial Library vaults each night?"

"He kept them overnight in a fireproof file at his house. Locked."

"Mr. Ainsworth, Haruki's suspicions sound a bit thin," James Lee commented. "I wonder why Haruki made no mention of the missing document at the inquest."

"It was not a missing document at that time. One of the filing clerks at the library discovered the absence of the document after the inquest."

"What do you want me to do, Mr. Ainsworth?"

"I want you to investigate Howard Lin."

"How do you think I had better proceed?" James Lee asked blandly.

"First of all, if I may presume to suggest a method to you, I would get the story straight from the Japanese."

"Why don't you have your local police work on it?" James Lee asked.

Harvey Ainsworth shook his head. “I'm afraid they'd be a bit out of their depth with ancient Chinese manuscripts and the Oriental mind. 'For ways that are dark,' if you will pardon the quotation.”

James Lee smiled and then with a quick decision, “I will have a talk with Haruki,” he said. “I will call at the university tomorrow at ten o'clock. Will you arrange for Haruki to meet me at your office at that hour?”

“He will be there waiting for you at that hour,” Harvey Ainsworth promised.

At James Lee's invitation, Harvey Ainsworth was present during Lee's interview with Haruki.

Looking straight at the Japanese, “Mr. Ainsworth tells me that you suspect that Professor Markham was murdered,” James Lee said.

Quietly, “I have reason to believe that to be the truth,” Haruki answered. “May I ask you to hold my information in confidence?”

Lee nodded. “Naturally.”

“It is not a quick story,” Haruki began. “First of all, we know that Professor Markham died from poison. That poison was available in the professor's house. He had enough of it to kill a thousand men in the chemical supplies in his photographic laboratory. On the evening of the professor's death while I was at work in the kitchen of his house I could not help but overhear his conversation with his Chinese assistant, Howard Lin. Lin was at work on a verbal translation of one of the manuscripts brought back from the last expedition in China. He read paragraphs of the manuscript in an even voice until suddenly he came upon something that served to excite him. The professor's interest and excitement seemed to increase at the same time.”

“Do you recall any of the text that occasioned the professor's excitement?”

“I remember some of it. I will try to quote from memory. 'On this felicitous occasion the clouds of heaven congealed. The trees of the high mountains glittered with a dew of precious stones. The trees trembled when the gods spoke and the mountains received the stones. The earth seized and concealed the stones for thousands of years and heaven wept in happiness when Wu

Wang was proclaimed ruler of the empire. On this happy day the precious stones locked in the high mountains were transported on the streams of heaven's tears to earth's treasury where two rivers meet, a day's journey east of the temple where Wu Wang spoke his vows of fealty to the people before he ascended to the jade throne...." That is the substance of the quotation from the manuscript that excited Professor Markham and Howard Lin so much."

Smiling at Haruki, "I must compliment you on the accuracy of your memory," James Lee said. He turned forthwith to address Harvey Ainsworth. "I wish you would telephone the police department and ask them to have an officer arrest Howard Lin and bring him in here immediately."

Ainsworth nodded. "Lin is probably over at the Chinese department. We'll have him arrested wherever he is."

"Thank you." James Lee turned again to Haruki. "I think you have an exceptional memory. And your deductions have been most interesting. As a matter of fact, you have cleared up the case considerably in my mind."

"You believe, then, Mr. Lee, as I do?" Haruki asked quickly.

"What do you believe?"

"If I may presume to suggest it, there is no remaining doubt as to the motive in the case."

"And that motive?"

Haruki hesitated. "A treasure in precious stones, of course. A treasure waiting a day's journey east of the temple where Wu Wang ascended to the jade throne—possession of that manuscript is just like having millions of dollars worth of diamonds and emeralds and rubies handed to you as a gift from the gods of Fortune."

James Lee contemplated the end of his cigarette. "Well, of course, that's one way of looking at it," he said. "I hadn't considered it in that light.... Of course, that would supply a motive. You assume, Haruki, that Lin killed the professor so that the detailed information as to the location of this treasure would belong exclusively to Lin?"

The smile on Haruki's face gave place to gravity. "Exactly," he said.

"You make it all very clear," James Lee complimented.

"Does Lin know that you overheard his translation?"

"I think not."

Interrupting the scene, Harvey Ainsworth's secretary came into the office. "There is a police officer out here. He has Howard Lin with him," the secretary said.

Ainsworth nodded. "Have them come in."

After his introduction to the officer who held Howard Lin in custody, "I have been doing a little work on the Markham case," James Lee explained. "Haruki here has some very interesting ideas relative to the case. He believes that Professor Markham was murdered.... I may add that I also believe that the professor was murdered."

He turned to Howard Lin. "Do you happen to remember the text of the legend of Wu Wang's treasure?"

"Of course I remember it," Howard Lin said sullenly. "Where is the Chinese scholar who doesn't know at least ten variations of that legend?"

"Could you recite it for me from memory following the line beginning, 'On this happy day'—?"

"The earlier versions or one of the later revisions?"

James Lee lifted his eyebrows. "I do not recall important variations in that section of the text."

At this, looking intently at James Lee, "Please accept my apologies," Howard Lin said quickly. "In you I recognized a countryman. Now I am happy to make appropriate obeisance to a Chinese scholar." A new light had replaced the sullen fear in Howard Lin's eyes.

"Please favor us with a recital of the text continuing from the line that begins, 'On this happy day.'"

Easily and without hesitation, continuing the quotation, Howard Lin recited the requested paragraph: "'On this happy day the precious stones locked in the high mountains were transported by the streaming tears of Heaven to Earth's treasury where three rivers meet, a three days' journey west of the palace where Wu Wang spoke his vows of fealty to his people before he ascended to the jade throne.'"

"Thank you, Mr. Lin." James Lee bowed to his countryman. "That is the text of the Wen Hien Tung Kao of the thirteenth century, isn't it? It seems to me that 'Heaven's streaming tears' was written 'the streams of Heaven's tears' in the earlier versions."

Howard Lin's face lighted with sincere pleasure. "Will you permit me to express my deep admiration?"

Frowning at this, dismissing the compliment, Lee turned to Ota Haruki and extended his cigarette case to the Japanese. "Have a cigarette," he invited, and then speaking again to Howard Lin, "Mr. Haruki is familiar with part of the legend, but has not had our facilities for studying the ancient texts. For instance, he remembers the treasure as being located where two rivers meet one day's journey east of the temple where Wu Wang spoke his vows."

To the Japanese, "You have it *east* instead of *west*, Haruki. *One* day's journey instead of *three*. *Two* rivers meeting instead of *three*. With those discrepancies in your sailing directions I am afraid you could spend your life in the Takla Makan without discovering the treasures of Wu Wang.... However, your recital was very interesting.... Why do you suppose Professor Markham and Mr. Lin became so greatly excited during the translation of the missing manuscript?"

Scowling, "It is natural for any man to become excited when millions in treasure lie within his grasp."

To Howard Lin, "Was that the reason for your excitement?"

"Naturally not," Lin said quietly. "But there was good reason for our enthusiasm. Do you remember, Mr. Lee, the date of the earliest existing text of the legend of Wu Wang's treasure?"

"I am not sure, but I think it is the Ling Soon text, dated early in the seventh century."

Howard Lin nodded. "Your memory is excellent. The missing manuscript that Professor Markham brought back with him, the manuscript that I was translating the night the professor died, dated two hundred years earlier than the Ling Soon text! It was written during the reign of the first of the Sung rulers! It antedates the Ling Soon text more than two hundred years!... You can understand Professor Mark-ham's delight—our excited mood."

James Lee turned to Ota Haruki. "You seem to have been mistaken in one important detail of your analysis. A regrettable error, Haruki. The manuscript was a scholar's treasure—of no intrinsic value. Incidentally, if the thief who killed Professor Markham desired to conceal the missing manuscript, where do you suppose he would hide it?"

Haruki's face was suddenly suffused with a surge of blood from his raging heart.

"Why do you ask me that question?" he grated. "How should I know...."

"I will ask you some simpler questions," James Lee interrupted. "When you smoke a cigarette do you always keep your left arm so close to your body? Do you think the thief who poisoned Professor Markham might hide the manuscript in the lining of his coat? By any chance does the lining of your coat conceal the missing manuscript?"

Haruki leaped to his feet, his face livid with rage. "You Chinese devil!" he snarled. He lunged at James Lee, a knife gleaming in his hand.

"You seem to—have lost—your Oriental—composure," James Lee suggested, combining four adroit bits of defense and attack with his suggestion.

Choking for breath and with his right arm twisted in James Lee's wrenching grip, Haruki dropped his knife.

James Lee nodded to the police officer who had sprung forward to help him. "Handcuffs," he said briefly, and then to Haruki, "You have the manuscript with you?" he asked.

"Yes, you damned snake!" Haruki panted.

"Sewed into the lining of the left sleeve of your coat." James Lee's exploring fingers stopped. "I was off a bit in that guess. Permit me to put your knife to a legitimate use."

When the missing manuscript had been ripped out of its hiding place, "There is one thing you may still do at this late moment to regain the Middle Pathway," James Lee suggested to the cringing Japanese. "You poisoned Professor Markham. You found the cyanide crystals in his photographic laboratory. You substituted a hydrocyanic solution for the harmless prescription from Ehrmann's Pharmacy. You poisoned him! You killed him! Confess your guilt!"

Haruki bowed his head. "Yes," he whispered, "I killed him."

James Lee turned to Harvey Ainsworth. "That seems to close the case," he said. He glanced down at Haruki. "It is regrettable that this poor fool should have confused the precious Wu Wang manuscript with common treasures of earth."

SCORNED WOMAN

In San Francisco, behind the scenes in the Green Moon Theater, working at a make-up box in the thin light of two fragrant candles, the Demon of Darkness, Gin Chow, a Shanghai man, painted his face with the traditional black and vermilion lineaments of his role. Six feet away from him, seated on a costume chest, Rose Irwin, slim and beautiful, sketched this bit of the scene backstage to the mild annoyance of the Demon of Darkness. When her color notes were complete the girl went on to one of the dressing rooms wherein, sprawled on a pile of costume chests, half a dozen servants of the actors lay drugged with the fumes of the third-grade opium with which their masters supplied them.

A single yellow bulb furnished the faint illumination for this scene. The girl, sketching rapidly, confined her work to the distorted faces of her subjects. She had finished the countenance of the fourth man from a favorable angle when a message whispered by a Chinese woman interrupted her.

"You must leave at once," the Chinese woman advised. "The Master of the Chests forbids your presence."

Rose Irwin frowned at the Chinese woman for a moment and then surrendered. "Thank you," she said. She hid her sketch block quickly under her coat and walked rapidly along the narrow passageway to the stairs that led back of the stage box. Here, pausing a moment to survey the several dark forms standing in the aisle that led to the foyer of the theater, she dropped a narrow veil across her eyes from the brim of her blue felt hat and walked forward resolutely toward the entrance of the theater.

On the street she turned directly toward her apartment in Ross Alley. She entered Ross Alley from Jackson Street. At a weather-beaten doorway she turned into the comparative sanctuary of the darkness that obscured a flight of stairs that led to the second story of the battered old building. In her studio her Chinese maid greeted her.

"Two Chinese men here while you were gone," the maid said. "They were bad men. I am afraid for you."

Rose Irwin handed her coat to the Chinese girl. She smiled at the girl. "Is it proper that a tigress should be afraid of rabbits?... Please pour me a cup of tea."

On the first night of the First Moon, San Francisco Chinatown picked up a little momentum in the early stages of its annual celebration.

Two hours after midnight a plane roared down out of the dark sky forty miles south of San Francisco. The plane made a perfect three-point landing on the first fairway of the Los Altos golf course. From a long, black touring car that waited on the open road that parallels the first fairway two men trotted toward the plane. Forthwith, across a hundred feet of turf that separated the plane from the touring car, these two men, aided by the pilot of the plane, carried three heavy boxes from the plane to the car.

The driver of the ear cackled a quick command to the pilot of the plane. Speaking in guttural Cantonese, "Make haste," he said. "Return to your sanctuary. You have done well."

In Chinatown four hours before dawn, while the local night was tortured with the din of exploding strings of firecrackers, the black touring car slowed to a stop in front of the Double Blessing butcher shop. The Dragon, eating the thin stars of the night for his first meal of the New Year, retreated in a gray dawn that revealed a wet street blotched with a crimson debris of shattered firecrackers. An hour after the dawn of the first day of the First Moon, Grant Avenue had quieted down.

Thirty feet from where Ross Alley opens into Jackson Street the huddled form of a dead man lay in the gutter.

"He's a Chinaman about forty years old," a member of the Chinatown squad reported to the desk sergeant over the telephone. "Nothing on him for identification. None of these local Chinks seem to know him."

"Bring him in," the desk sergeant ordered. "How was he killed?"

"He was shot in the back."

"Shot or stabbed?"

"Listen, Cap, you never seen a knife hot enough to singe a man's coat, did you?"

"Bring him in," the desk sergeant said.

In the Cave of Harmony, twenty feet under Grant Avenue, gravity marked the countenance of old Sung Kong. Facing four of the elders of Chinatown, he removed his heavy silver spectacles. "Tsao-sui-liao," he whispered. "We have met with disaster! I suggested to you a year ago that it were better to endure persecution than to follow depraved courses."

"We will not forget the benefits conferred by your wisdom," one of the old Chinese men answered presently. "I must remind you that this is a world of darkness. Under your former plan seven of our brothers in the Central Glory were destroyed."

Sung Kong nodded slowly. "You are of clear perception," he said to his critic. "I admit that we have failed. There is but one recompense to virtue."

"Enough!" A third member of the group banged an empty porcelain wine cup down on the teakwood table. "Enough of yesterday. There is no help for it. As one practical suggestion whereby we may regain the lost harmony, enjoy sweet after bitter, I suggest that we present our problem to the genius who serves the American government."

"Our countryman, James Lee Wong?"

The old man nodded. "We cannot forget that more than once he has led us out of the place of death."

A cackling chorus of approving voices followed. Old Sung Kong nodded. "I will ask our countryman, James Lee, to serve us once again," he said. "I will transfer the burden of our problem to his shoulders."

In the library of James Lee's apartment, greeting the Chinese operative of the Department of Justice, old Sung Kong, following the Ritual of Right Conduct, removed his silver-bowed spectacles and shook hands with himself three times. "Long life, great wealth," Sung Kong said in Cantonese. Then, fitting his language to the locale of his problem, "I hope you enjoy the Eight Blessings."

At this, bowing to the elder man, after a quick mental review of the Eight Blessings, James Lee smiled. "The eighth blessing is unattainable," he reminded Sung Kong. "I enjoy at least five of them." .

"Faithful wife, dutiful sons?"

James Lee shook his head. "You know that I have yet to enjoy six and seven. Will you have wine?"

"Presently. At the moment the realm of my intellect is sufficiently foggy without obscuring it with the vapors of wine."

"Life is a labyrinth. Your feet have strayed from the Middle Pathway?"

The old man nodded slowly. "My weary feet have lost the Central Pathway," he admitted. "I have come to ask your guidance."

"How can the eyebrows of youth compare with the beard of age?"

"Thou art of clear perception. The elder council in this colony of your countrymen here in the land of the foreign devils enjoyed communion in the Cave of Harmony. I am delegated to ask you to aid us."

James Lee reached for a cigarette. "What is your problem?" he asked, speaking gently to the troubled Sung Kong.

"You know of our interest in the affairs in the Central Glory?" Sung Kong asked.

For a moment a whimsical smile lighted the corners of James Lee's mouth. Before he could speak, "Accept my apologies for that question," Sung Kong requested. "To open my heart let me say that among the contributions to the war chest of government not the least important are the various sums of money remitted by my associates in the Cave of Harmony. Our latest project has failed. Fang Yut engineered it."

"You mean that he bought the opium Gin Chow shipped to Mexico last month? The stuff that was brought up by airplane?"

Sung Kong nodded. "Fang Yut arranged for the purchase," he admitted. "Two hundred thousand dollars is no mean sum of money."

"Is that why Gin Chow was murdered?"

"Could there be another reason?"

James Lee frowned. "Gin Chow was notoriously an agent of the Nanking government."

"Your words are adorned with truth," Sung Kong admitted. "Nevertheless we think that Gin Chow was killed by a common thief. On the night that Fang Yut collected the money for the opium shipment he gave it to Gin Chow. He undertook to guard Gin Chow to the Cave of Harmony."

"Where was the money paid over to Gin Chow?" James Lee asked.

"In Fang Yut's residence."

"Do you mean his apartment over the Double Blessing butcher shop?"

"That was where Gin Chow received the money."

"What does Fang Yut say?"

"His testimony to the agents of the police department is simple enough. A man with a drawn revolver confronted Fang Yut and Gin Chow in Ross Alley near Jackson Street. Gin Chow naturally attempted to defend himself. Forthwith he was killed."

"Shot in the back as I remember," James Lee observed. "Retreat was never Gin Chow's idea of defense."

Sung Kong's eyes narrowed. "When Fang Yut recovers it might be well to question him further about that detail."

"Fang Yut is ill?" James Lee asked blandly.

Old Sung Kong nodded. "The demons of torture have invaded his body."

James Lee's level glance lifted to a clock on the mantel over the fireplace in his library. "I will be glad to help you with your problem," he said quickly. "You will excuse me now." An air of impatience marked his words. "Time is an arrow."

With mild, disgruntled surprise at the quick termination of the conference, old Sung Kong got to his feet. "Good luck, long life," he said quickly to the federal operative. Making a final obeisance at the entrance, "Seven sons to mourn at your grave," the elder Chinese concluded, shaking hands with himself three times.

James Lee smiled. "Can't you think of anything more cheerful than a grave?" he asked, violating the Ritual of Right Conduct.

Old Sung Kong blinked. "Eight Blessings," he mumbled, shuffling away toward the street that led to the Cave of Harmony.

The street doors of the Double Blessing butcher shop were closed when James Lee arrived. Twenty feet from the main entrance of the shop, north on Grant Avenue, on a door which opened to a stairway leading to Fang Yut's living rooms above his store, two streamers of white cotton cloth bore replicas painted in vermilion ink of Fang Yut's family names.

Following an interval of two minutes after James Lee had knocked on the door, "What do you desire?" a voice asked from within.

"I am Fang Yut's friend," James Lee said.

"Your name?"

James Lee spoke his name. The door opened. "You are welcome to this house of sorrow," one of Fang Yut's servants on sentinel duty recited in a hollow voice.

"The Dragon...."

"My master ascended on the Dragon on the fourth hour of morning."

"The priests?"

"My mistress, Lily Fang, will have no traffic with the agents of the Seventh Heaven."

"The unimportant journey—Fang Yut returns to earth to sleep in his grave on the third seventh day?"

"Old ways are forgotten," the servant answered. "Tomorrow the shell of my master's spirit will be transported to its earthly sanctuary."

"Where is the place of burial?"

"Presently my master will sleep close beside the graves of his ancestors. For a little while he will wait in his tomb on the southern slope of Sleeping Willow Hill."

"Your mistress, the lady Lily Fang?"

"She is prostrate with sorrow at my master's passing."

After a moment, with a quick glance at the sentinel servant of Fang Yut's house, "Here is a dollar," James Lee said. "Enjoy a libation of good black wine." He handed the man a dollar bill. "On the official documents relating to the deplorable event what reason was assigned for Fang Yut's death?"

"The white doctors decided that my master died from an overdose of opium. It was so recorded," the servant answered. "Long life, seven sons." The sentinel servant bowed low.

James Lee smiled. “Enjoy your wine. After a typhoon there are plums to gather.”

Fang Yut's funeral seemed to James Lee to be mildly spectacular.

When the limousine carrying Lily Fang passed the window through which James Lee was observing the parade of death he noted that no tears lay below the closed lids of the widow's eyes. He stepped outdoors quickly and, still observing the grief-stricken Lily Fang, he elbowed his way through the throng, keeping the grieving woman well in view. Suddenly, as if surfeited with the calisthenics of her grief, Lily Fang opened her eyes. She reached her smooth, white hand with its slim, tapering fingers out toward a maid who crouched at her feet. James Lee saw her select a shred of candied coconut from a little wicker basket that the maid had held up to her. Lily Fang permitted her slim white hand to convey the sweetmeat to her vermilion lips. Then, closing her eyes, she resigned herself again to her wailing and to the sorrowful job of rolling her head from side to side.

“Coconut candy!” James Lee reflected. “Lily Fang and her false tears!” After a moment, “If a woman loves a man she does not gorge herself on coconut candy on the way to his grave.... Lily Fang's tears of grief are phony!”

James Lee missed one important incident in the progress of the funeral procession. Half a block from the portals of the Stockton Street tunnel the parade, turning north on Stockton Street, was halted for a moment by a brawl that centered about a slim American girl. The girl was Rose Irwin and the occasion for the melee was her attempt to photograph the funeral procession of Fang Yut. From a packing box in the front of Moy Gow's store the girl made five exposures with her camera, shooting variously Lily Fang and her decorated limousine, the hired mourners, the hearse and the twelve trailing priests behind this vehicle of death.

A sudden clash between two Chinese at Rose Irwin's feet spread until ten struggling men were involved. Crashing into the packing case on which she stood, the fighting crew dethroned the slim girl in one surging rush. A Chinese man helped her to her feet. Thirty seconds later, from a point twenty feet away from the girl, another Chinese elbowed his way to her side. In his hand he held the broken remains of the camera that she had used. “More better you not stay here,” the man said in pidgin, handing Rose Irwin her camera.

When she had returned to her studio she opened the camera. The roll of film was missing.

Bringing her mistress a glass of brandy, “Two more bad men came to see you,” the maid announced. “One man said very good if you leave San Francisco....”

The American girl frowned at her servant. “You are a silly fool,” she said sharply. “Please make me a cup of tea.”

At six o'clock in the evening of the day of Fang Yut's funeral, in his library James Lee called quickly to his house boy. Emphasis derived from a sudden decision marked his words. “I will not be here for dinner tonight. Bring me a heavy overcoat. Telephone Mr. Decker to come over here. Ask him to wait here until he hears from me.”

The servant bowed. After a moment's silence, “What time will you come back?” he asked.

“Somewhere around midnight,” James Lee said, putting on his coat. “If I don't come back tonight fix the guest room for Mr. Decker.”

From his apartment James Lee walked rapidly to a garage half a block away, where he kept his car. He drove directly to the Green Moon Theater. When he had parked his car he entered the theater and made his way backstage. Here for three hours, mingling with the cast, he listened variously to the shrieking music, the falsetto voices and the clanging gongs that bored through the lines and business of a seemingly interminable play involving the suspicious husband in the pear garden. At eleven o'clock, during a moment when Ping Kuei, the beggar, sang of the day within the garden when his lady love divine, daughter of a wealthy noble, “promised that she would be mine,” James Lee with marked abruptness terminated a sketchy conversation with the man who had replaced the dead Gin Chow. “It is futile to wish you long life,” James Lee said caustically to this man. “More appropriately let me wish you good luck.... good night.”

Midnight found James Lee at the portals of the Chinese cemetery. Sleeping Willow Hill was shrouded with drifting wraiths of fog borne in from the cold Pacific. He made his way along a road lined with drooping cedars until he came to the tombs of the Wong family. Here, remembering the site that Fang Yut had picked for his own last resting place, he turned to the left across a turf soft with the first grasses of spring, electing to traverse this more direct route rather than to follow the roadway which led around the south slope of Sleeping Willow Hill. When he was a hundred feet away from Fang Yut's tomb he halted at the sound of a man's voice raised in angry exclamation. He heard eleven cackling syllables in the Cantonese dialect. "You fool! Trust a woman to ignore a warning! This will be the end of your interference." There followed a woman's scream of anguish, and then this was muffled quickly to silence.

Ten seconds later the flaring beams of an automobile's headlights stabbed through the drifting fog.

"Someone seems to have beaten me to my first move in this game," James Lee reflected. "A woman!"

He heard the snarling gears of the starter and then the roaring exhaust of the car's engine. "Kidnapped—they've got her! That means more trouble."

He was eighty feet from the road around Sleeping Willow Hill when the car roared past him, racing toward the main highway. He remained quiet for four minutes after the car had gone and then he resumed his silent approach to Fang Yut's tomb. Twenty feet away from the portals of the ornamented structure he risked a three-second flash from an electric light that he carried. The door of Fang Yut's tomb was open. Without fear now, sensing the fact that Fang Yut's place of sepulcher was deserted, he stepped quickly to the side of the heavy coffin. He swung the piercing ray of his flashlight toward it. Fang Yut's coffin was empty.

"This affair is becoming a bit complicated," James Lee reflected, starting back toward his car.

In the library of his apartment at one o'clock in the morning, greeting his associate, John Decker, who had been sleeping on the long couch fronting the fireplace, "Dash over to Fang Yut's joint and find out where his widow is," James Lee directed. "I mean Lily Fang—she was his number one wife. Get back here right away."

Decker nodded. "Check.... Wait a minute. I'm still half asleep.... There was a Chinese girl called in here to see you an hour ago. I tried to hold her but she insisted on returning to her own place."

"Who was she?"

"She works for this American girl, Rose Irwin, the painter who lives here in Chinatown—the sweet little state narcotic operative."

"What did she want?"

"She wanted you to find Rose Irwin for her. She said she was afraid that some of Fang Yut's outfit might have moved in on the little lady."

James Lee scowled, and from his scowl it was evident that he believed that the fears of Rose Irwin's servant were not without a basis of probability. The scream he had heard at Fang Yut's tomb! He nodded quickly at Decker. "Fair enough! Round up the dope about Lily Fang and get back here on the run!"

John Decker came back with his report in eighteen minutes. "Under the terms of Fang Yut's will Lily Fang was sold to Gat Mow. You know him, don't you?"

The federal operative nodded. "You forget that I dug up the evidence that socked him eight years ago in the white slave case. Has Lily Fang moved out of her house?"

"She headed for Stockton ten hours ago."

James Lee scowled at the telephone on his desk for twenty seconds. Then with a quickened animation in his voice, "You know what Gat Mow is doing now, don't you?" he asked.

Decker nodded. "Running a gambling joint on an ark boat somewhere in the Stockton delta. Is that right?"

"That's part of his game. He bought the old Six Pleasures a year ago and rigged it up with a couple of added attractions. He's branched out with two more rackets besides gambling. I had a report on him a month ago. His big money still comes from his fan-tan game but lately he has been able to supply his customers with hop and women.... Listen to me, boy, we've got to move in on Gat Mow tonight! Have you got your guns with you?"

"I've got 'em both," Decker answered.

"You will need them," James Lee said.

The Six Pleasures, which had been lately renamed the "Ting Cho"—"Pavilion of Luxury"—was an eighty-foot scow drawing a scant three feet.

Five hours after midnight, with John Decker in the stern of a skiff that he had borrowed from some unknown owner who had moored it on the west bank of Middle River, James Lee rowed a thousand feet downstream from Lady Island to where the Ting Cho lay.

Quietly to John Decker as they neared the Ting Cho, "Remember the play," James Lee repeated. "Don't blast unless you have to. We go into the gambling-room through that door on the forward deck. Keep everybody covered until I get the bracelets on Gat Mow. If he's in his own quarters on the upper deck you may have to come up and lend me a hand, because it's a million to one that Fang Yut will be with him."

"I got you," Decker said. "I still think there's mighty slim evidence back of your theory that Fang Yut is alive."

"Lily Fang wasn't drowning any real tears in candied coconut," James Lee protested. "I know Chinese women better than you do.... All right, hop to it! Up you go.... Here, make her fast to the rail."

The thin whining strains of a Chinese banjo played by a slave girl furnished the overture for John Decker's entrance into the gambling-room of the Ting Cho. At this early hour of the morning the gambling play had quieted, but twenty patrons still remained at the fan-tan table.

Decker walked into the scene with his hands down. Ten feet beyond the entrance door he leveled two black automatics at the players around the fan-tan table. "This is not a hold-up," he said evenly, barely loud enough for the assemblage to hear him. Then over his shoulder to James Lee, "Make it snappy, Chief," he called. "I think you've got Gat Mow at the table.... Up at the head end with that Filipino girl."

"That's him." James Lee walked quickly to Gat Mow's side. "Hands behind you!"

Gat Mow smiled thinly at James Lee. "Good evening, traitor," he said. "Why must you...."

"Shut up! This is a time for silence!" A pair of handcuffs clicked about Gat Mow's wrists. "The keys to your rooms?"

"This is a time for silence," Gat Mow repeated, sneering at his captor.

"And action." A preliminary exploration of Gat Mow's raiment brought forth a stubby, short-barreled, blue .38 and a bunch of keys. "You wait here," James Lee said to Gat Mow. "If you move, my man will shoot you." To John Decker, "Hold everybody right here. I'm going topside."

James Lee walked quietly up the narrow stairway that led to the upper deck. At the head of the stairs he turned to his right. With a preliminary greeting, imitating Gat Mow's voice as best he could, he tried the heavy door that led to Gat Mow's private rooms. To his surprise the door was unlocked. As it opened, from within he heard a harsh challenge. The voice was Fang Yut's voice. James Lee leveled the gun in his right hand at the shadowed sanctuary of a bunk built into the west wall of the cabin. A woman screamed and in the high falsetto of her alarm James Lee recognized Lily Fang.

"Fang Yut, move and I kill you!" James Lee said. "Stand up! This is the first hour of your destruction."

"I will return the money," Fang Yut began. "I will pay you...."

"You will pay for killing Gin Chow with your life!" James Lee interrupted. Then, "Where is the white girl?"

Fang Yut scowled. "I have no traffic in white girls."

Instantly, spending a venomous jealousy in one screaming accusation, "He lies!" Lily Fang said. "The woman is in that room!"

James Lee nodded toward Lily Fang. "When this typhoon blows over there will be ripe pears for you to gather," he promised, speaking in Cantonese. Covering Fang Yut with his gun James Lee reached into the side pocket of his overcoat for a pair of handcuffs. He threw the jingling steel at Lily Fang's feet. "Hold your hands in front of you," he said to Fang Yut, and then to Lily Fang, "Chain him to the bars of that window.... Press them tight around his wrists.... Thank you. A dutiful wife is her husband's greatest treasure."

Still wary, reluctant to turn away from his captive, James Lee walked to his left, to the locked door of the room wherein Rose Irwin was imprisoned. The fourth key that he tried from the dangling collection of Gat Mow's key ring fitted the lock. The heavy door swung inward. In the obscurity of the unlighted room James Lee saw the figure of the slim American girl lying inert on a couch in the corner. He called to her, "Miss Irwin!"

There was no reply.

Intervening to calm James Lee's fears, "She is unharmed," Lily Fang assured him. "She is not hurt—but Fang Yut drugged her tea. She will wake up after the first hour of daylight."

At nine o'clock, fully conscious after her perilous sleeping, "I can never thank you, Mr. Lee, for what you've done!" Rose Irwin said.

James Lee smiled at the girl. "You can do two things for me," he began. "As the first expression of your gratitude I would like to have you resign from the state narcotic bureau as soon as we get to San Francisco."

Rose Irwin frowned at her companion. "But I love the work," she protested. "It is fascinating. You will forgive me if I boast a bit—I broke the Headland case single-handed. I rounded up the Revell outfit after your people had let them escape. I trailed Walter Crow from Sacramento to Honduras—and brought him back alive. There was the...."

Interrupting the recital, James Lee lifted his hand. "Permit me to make my second request. After you resign your state narcotic job I want you to make one quick jump to the Department of Justice. You're the smartest woman I ever knew. We need you in our business."

"I'll give the department the best I have," Rose Irwin answered in delighted acceptance....

In the Cave of Harmony twenty feet under Grant Avenue, with old Sung Keng beside him, James Lee faced seven of the elder governors of San Francisco's Chinatown. "I have decided to give the Nanking government the funds which you derived from your unworthy enterprise," he announced. "The United States government holds Gat Mow a prisoner. The opium that went to the burial place in Fang Yut's coffin has been destroyed. Any further participation on your part in the opium traffic will mean that all of you will end your lives in a federal prison.

Finally, in the interests of justice I shall surrender Fang Yut to you. He has confessed to me that he killed Gin Chow."

"He probably killed the man that lay dead in his house when the coroner came," old Sung Kong interrupted.

"Perhaps that is true," James Lee answered. "Fang Yut did not confess to that ... I have one favor to ask of you—when the moment comes for Fang Yut to bid farewell to life...."

"One thousand slices of his flesh—slow with a small knife so that he may suffer ten thousand years of torture," a kindly-faced ancient of Chinatown suggested.

"A quick death with the drug of sleep," James Lee countered. "I demand that you do not use the ancient methods of torture."

After a moment's deliberation old Sung Kong nodded slowly. "It shall be as you desire."

There was another longer period of silence broken finally by the thin, rasping voice of the fragile old Wang Lin. "The American painter girl?" Wang Lin asked. "Is she still to be numbered with the annoying insects of this region?"

"She has resigned her job with the state narcotic bureau," James Lee announced, ornamenting the gold of truth with the brass of fact.

Old Wang Lin smiled thinly. "She has attained wisdom at an early age," he commented. "Hola! Now that the storm has passed let us enjoy a cup of wine."

SEVEN OF SPADES

Over Arizona, eighty miles east of the California line, the pilot of the Silver Arrow came back into the cabin of the plane with a message for James Lee. James Lee read the message:

BANCROFT ON DUTCH FLINT CASE MURDERED STOP YOUR ORDERS OMAHA CANCELLED STOP CALL ME LONG DISTANCE FROM STANTON

The message was signed by the chief of the Bureau of Investigation. James Lee looked up at the pilot of the Silver Arrow. "You'll set me down at Stanton?"

The pilot nodded. "I'll land you there in thirty minutes, Mr. Lee.... Wasn't Bancroft the young fellow who rode out with me about a month ago? Slim and red-headed? Mining engineer?"—

"You have a good memory."

"Was he a G-man?"

James Lee frowned. "Mr. Bancroft was a mining engineer.... Please remember that this message from the Department is strictly confidential."

The pilot nodded. "I get you. Good luck. I'll set her down at Stanton for you in less than half an hour."

From Washington, speaking to James Lee at Stanton over long distance, "Bancroft was undercover at Redstone," the chief said. "Ranger. Park service. Lived in a cabin with another ranger by the name of Al Blake. Sheriff Deane figures that Blake is the killer. He has him jailed at Stanton."

"What's the latest you have on Dutch Flint?"

"We think he's hiding north of Redstone."

"You're sending me the file on the case?"

"It's on a westbound plane right now. If you get a line on Flint you'd better have some of your men over from Los Angeles and San Francisco."

"What about Blake?"

"Bancroft figured he was a good egg.... Have a talk with Sheriff Deane right away and hop to it. That's all—and good luck."

After he had introduced himself to Sheriff Deane, "I guess you don't need any help on this case, Sheriff," James Lee began, "but Frank Bancroft was a pal of mine in the service. We worked together for seven or eight years and I have a personal interest in putting the man who killed him on the spot."

"I'm mighty glad to have you on the job, Mr. Lee. I guess there ain't much work for you to do. We've got the deadwood on Al Blake." The sheriff scowled. "If I ain't mistaken I'll get a confession out of him by six o'clock tonight."

"I'd like to talk to him."

"Go ahead. Help yourself."

James Lee was silent for a moment and then, "Sheriff, do you remember the details of Dutch Flint's record?"

"Dutch Flint—I can't say that I do. A big-time gangster, wasn't he?"

"He still is. Dutch Flint and his mob blasted a few country banks in Kansas and Missouri for a while and then they got into the big money on a kidnapping case. You remember the Matson snatching, don't you?"

"I'm kinda cloudy on that. Matson was a young feller?"

"Matson was thirty years old. They killed him. The second set of headlines covered the Melville girl kidnapping. They killed her. That was a year ago. We captured three of the gang but Dutch Flint got away.... Would you say offhand, Sheriff, that Al Blake might be one of Dutch Flint's new outfit?"

"No! Al Blake ain't nuthin' but a hot-headed young ranger. He's been up at Redstone there for six or eight months. He's been in the park service for the last ten years."

"What was his motive in killing Bancroft?"

"The best motive in the world. Jealousy."

"Jealousy—do you mean that there's a woman in the case?"

"No. Professional jealousy. Bancroft come in with sixty dollars a month more on his pay check than Blake got. Blake was headed for promotion until Bancroft showed up."

"Just plain professional jealousy—and a hot temper."

The sheriff nodded. "That's it exactly."

"I'll have a talk with Blake."

To the deputy sheriff who escorted him to Al Blake's cell, "Let me in the cell and then leave us," James Lee directed. Smiling, "You never can make 'em talk in front of witnesses."

The deputy understood. "I get you, Mr. Lee," he said. "Here he is."

Facing Al Blake, "I've come down to talk to you about my friend Frank Bancroft. I'm an operative for the Bureau of Investigation," the Chinese detective explained, introducing himself. "My name is James Lee."

Blake held out his hand. "I'm what's left of Al Blake, Mr. Lee. This thing has got me."

James Lee looked straight at the prisoner. "Did you kill Frank Bancroft?"

"No! Frank was the swellest guy I ever knew. All I can say is...."

Interrupting the prisoner, "How did Frank like his job?"

"Offhand, I'd say he was stuck on his job. He loved the country, Mr. Lee. We got along fine. One of the swellest partners in the world:"

"What time did you get back to the cabin—when you found Frank's body?"

"Close to suppertime—around six o'clock."

"What did you do when you walked into the cabin?"

"I saw Frank lying on the floor. I felt his heart ... he was dead."

"And then?"

"I dragged him over to his bunk, Mr. Lee, and lifted him up into it."

"Then what?"

"Then I went out and got a bucket of water and sloshed it on the floor to wash the blood away. It was right in the middle of the floor. When I came back with the water I saw that the staple on the door that we padlock the cabin with was busted."

"What did you do after you cleaned up the blood on the floor?"

"I didn't clean it up—I just heaved a bucket of water on it to wash it down through the cracks in the floor. The floor is rough boards with cracks half an inch wide. I went over to the telephone and called up the operator at Crystal and told him to get hold of Sheriff Deane. I told him to send somebody over from Crystal. It's only fifteen miles."

"How long did it take the sheriff to get to Redstone?"

"He didn't come. One of his deputies came over from Crystal and pinched me. I was plenty surprised and plenty sore."

James Lee nodded. "No doubt. What time were you arrested?"

"I didn't keep any track of the time after I found Frank's body, but I must have been arrested somewhere around seven o'clock that evening. They got me into jail here at Stanton before midnight."

"Who arrested you?"

"Bill Putnam. He's been one of Deane's deputies for three or four years."

"Who is Bill Putnam?"

"He runs a pool hall here in Stanton; sort of a cigar store and pool hall. I've been in it half a dozen times. There's generally a poker game running in the back end of the joint."

"What do you suppose Putnam was doing in Crystal?"

"He ranges around quite a lot. He's been gambling in prospect holes and gold mines and things like that on the side ever since he landed here."

"How long has he been in Stanton?"

"As near as I remember from what I heard he came here six or eight years ago. There was some sort of a story about some trouble he got into once in Reno. I never heard the straight of it. There was one more thing, Mr. Lee—when I walked into the cabin and saw Frank's body lying there—that is, when I went over to telephone—I remember the little desk we used was all mussed up."

"You mean somebody had gone through it?"

"Yes, sir, that's the way it looked."

"Where is this pool hall that Mr. Putnam runs?"

"It's a couple of blocks down the street from the courthouse."

"I'll have a talk with him. I'll see you later in the day," James Lee said.

The trace of a smile quivered in the corners of Al Blake's mouth. "I'll wait here for you," he said.

Impulsively James Lee held out his hand to the prisoner. "Keep your chin up."

The proprietor of the Pastime Club, Bill Putnam, was seated at a little desk against the back wall of the poolroom when James Lee entered the place. Three pool tables filled the central space of the long room. In the first apartment back of the poolroom a poker game was in progress; save for the proprietor, the large central room was empty.

Entering the place, "I'm looking for Mr. Putnam," James Lee said.

"My name is Putnam. What can I do for you?"

"My name is Lee, Bureau of Investigation. I want to talk to you about the Bancroft murder."

"Go ahead and talk. Have they lynched Al Blake yet?"

"Do you think Blake killed Bancroft?"

"It's a cinch."

"What makes you think so?"

"I'll spring my evidence in a trial court, unless Blake is strung up before then."

"You don't seem to be in a very pleasant humor this morning, Mr. Putnam."

"Why the hell should I be in a pleasant humor? The sheriff and I and the local courts can take care of our troubles without any of you smart boys from the outside butting into the game."

James Lee asked quietly, "Has anyone ever suggested to you that your deputy's badge isn't large enough to cover your Reno record?"

Bill Putnam got to his feet. "What do you mean?"

James Lee risked a small bet on Putnam's evident agitation at the mention of the Reno record. "I mean that some of the department's files are never closed.... I'd like to talk to you about the Bancroft murder if you don't mind. I'm friendly. How about it?"

Bill Putnam scowled. "Go ahead. What do you want to know?"

"Tell the story."

"There isn't much story. I was up in Crystal on business.

Sheriff Deane telephoned me that Bancroft had been murdered. I drove over to the cabin at Redstone and arrested Al Blake. Bancroft was dead. Blake had some blood on him. I covered Blake with my gun and got the handcuffs on him and brought him in. That was all there was to it."

"Did you bring Bancroft's body with you?"

"I was driving a little roadster. Ben Carver was in Crystal with a light truck. I told him to follow me over to Redstone and after I pinched Blake I told Carver to haul Bancroft's body down here to Stanton and turn it over to the coroner."

"Who is Carver?" James Lee asked.

"He runs a saddlery store up the street here. He sells Indian jewelry and rugs and things like that as a side line."

"Did you examine the cabin at Redstone for any evidence of the murder?"

"Evidence hell! The man was lying there dead! Nobody but Blake had been there with him. What better evidence do you want?"

Realizing the futility of the conversation, Lee nodded in feigned agreement.

"I guess you're right," he said. "Thanks. Where did you say Carver's place was?"

"Half a block up the street—west."

"Thank you, Mr. Putnam.... There is one other thing. Going over to the cabin at Redstone from Crystal, how far behind you was Ben Carver?"

"I didn't pay any attention to that. He was pretty close, I guess, till we got almost to Redstone. Then he dropped behind so that if there was any shooting I could take care of things single-handed."

"Is the road from Crystal to Redstone dusty?"

"It's solid rock most of the way. Good, clean rock. The wind blows too strong most of the time to let any dust lay around."

"Did you take Blake back to Crystal after you captured him?"

"No; I brought him straight south to Stanton. There's a sort of a side road from Redstone to Horn Spring where it hits the main road from Stanton to Crystal, about eighty miles up the line."

"And Carver brought Bancroft's body to Stanton over the same road?"

"Yep. He followed right behind me all the way."

"Thank you, Mr. Putnam. I'll see you again before I leave."

Putnam scowled. "So long," he said.

Marching down the long aisle of Ben Carver's pungent saddlery shop after a cracked bell had clanked in announcement of his entrance, James Lee found the proprietor of the place midway of the long building. Carver, engaged at the moment in opening a consignment of Navaho jewelry from a Connecticut manufacturer, looked up over his left shoulder.

"What can I do for you?" he said, smiling thinly at James Lee.

"I'd like to talk to you about Frank Bancroft's murder."

Carver frowned. "Why do you want to talk to me about that mess? You working for Al Blake?"'

"I'm working for the Department of Justice. Do you think Blake killed Bancroft?"

"Sure he did! There was nobody else in the cabin when me and Putnam got there."

"What motive did Blake have for killing Bancroft?"

"How the hell do I know why he killed him? Probably they were both nuts about the same girl.... You don't mind if I ask you a question or two, do you?"

James Lee nodded. "Go ahead."

"In the first place, where do you cut into this game? How does Bancroft rate a G-man at his inquest?"

"What else do you want to know?"

Carver picked up a turquoise ring that lay on the table in front of him. He looked at the ring for a moment and then, "Just to cut this short, how would you like to get the hell out of my place right now?" he asked.

James Lee reached for a cigarette and lighted it. "I wouldn't mind—but before I go I'd like to ask you two more questions."

The speaker took a long, deep drag at his cigarette and gazed at the ceiling for a moment. Then through a curling cloud of smoke, "Do you think you could stand up in court and clear yourself of an indictment for murder in case the district attorney got—troublesome?"

Ben Carver snorted. "Nuts to you! I'll come back with a question: Do you think you can live through the night?"

James Lee nodded. "Yes," he said, "I think I can!... I'll be at the Eagle Hotel tonight in case you want to make any suggestions about locating Bancroft's murderer."

Leaving the Carver establishment, James Lee walked directly to the sheriff's office in the courthouse.

To Sheriff Deane, "I want to take Blake up to Redstone with me tomorrow morning," he said. "I want you to release him into my custody tomorrow."

Joe Deane grunted. "How do I know that you'll get him back here?" he countered. "How do I know somebody won't take him off your hands and hang him?"

"I'll be responsible for the man," James Lee said coldly. "One more favor, Sheriff, if you don't mind. Have one of your men meet the night plane from the East. The Department is sending out some records that I need on this case."

The sheriff nodded. "Sure you trust us messenger boys, Mr. Lee?"

With some bitterness, "I'd trust you as messenger boys. If you really want to do me an important favor you might post a man or two around the Eagle Hotel tonight to see that I live till morning."

"You turning yellow?"

"Put it that way if you wish to."

An hour after sundown that night a bullet punctured a neat hole in the glass of a bedroom window in the Eagle Hotel. The bullet, whining on its futile way at short range, followed a trajectory that lay an inch above James Lee's left shoulder and an inch to the left of his neck.

One second thereafter James Lee's silhouette dropped from the lighted shade that veiled the window of his room.

At morning, after he had signed the document that gave him custody of Al Blake, looking straight at Sheriff Deane, "I'm grateful to you for letting one of your deputies ride herd on me last night. They almost got me."

"What do you mean—somebody shoot at you last night?"

"Let's say he shot in my general direction. If my shadow hadn't been six or eight inches taller than I happen to be, the Bancroft murder case would have been complicated with another corpse. I dug the bullet out of the wall of a bedroom three doors away from my room. Here it is."

Sheriff Deane looked mildly annoyed. "Doggone it, Mr. Lee, that's an awful crazy story to tell me this early after breakfast." He looked down at the battered bullet in the palm of his right hand. "I can't imagine who might have took a shot at you. What do you want me to do about it?"

"Nothing—but you might let me keep that bullet as a souvenir of your local hospitality.... Now if you'll turn Blake over to me I'll be on my way. I have a lot of work to do before sundown tonight."

At the door of the cabin where Frank Bancroft had been killed Al Blake halted for a moment. "That's the busted staple, Mr. Lee," he said. "See how this hasp is battered and bent?"

James Lee looked at the broken fastening of the door. "What about the lock? Was it found?"

"It was just a cheap little padlock. It broke before either the hasp or the staple gave way. I didn't see it when I first looked. Whoever broke into the place probably threw it away."

"We'll have a look for it after a while. Let's go inside.... Is that where you cleaned up the blood on the floor?"

Blake nodded solemnly.

James Lee surveyed the scene for a moment. Then, quickly, "Was that champagne bottle that you use for a candlestick tipped over on the desk the last time you saw it?"

"I don't remember."

Blake walked toward his desk.

"Don't touch that bottle. Wait a moment.... Did you or Bancroft happen to have any talcum powder in your shaving outfit?"

"Frank had some."

"Get it for me."

A moment later, on the dark green surface of the overturned bottle on the desk, James Lee sifted a cloud of talcum powder.. Then, "Hand me that shaving brush up there, will you?"

Very gently rotating the dark green bottle as he worked, James Lee brushed away the surplus powder on its surface.

When the whitened surface had grayed from its thinning dust of talc, he laid down the shaving brush. He began a close inspection of the surface of the bottle with an eight-power lens. After the lens had ranged across ten or fifteen square inches of the bottle's surface he halted suddenly and looked up at Al Blake.

"We've hit pay dirt!" James Lee said grimly. "Dutch Flint's fingerprints! The file on him came in last night from Washington. I memorized the high spots in his record. Here! Take this glass and look at that V-shaped scar that ties up the triangle and the loop. Index finger of Dutch Flint's right hand!"

"Dutch Flint? Where does that gangster come into this picture?"

"He probably comes in to save your life—and my reputation." Quickly then, "I've got a hunch!" James Lee reached in his pocket and pulled out the battered bullet that had been fired at him the night before. "I've overlooked a big bet!... Can I get Washington on this telephone?"

"She's probably still connected."

"What central?"

"Crystal. The switchboard is in the back end of the general store."

James Lee frowned. "I've got to take a chance." He took the receiver off the hook. He clicked the phone twice. "She's still alive." Then to the Crystal central, "Get me the chief of the Bureau of Investigation at Washington.... Official... Government rush."

"I'll call you back," central said.

"I'll wait on the line. Burn it through."

To the chief less than three minutes later, "James Lee talking. I got the file on the Matson, Melville, Continental man last night. Tell me something—quick.... Can you hear me?"

"Clear as a bell," the chief answered.

"Tell me this: What kind of a gun fired that bullet that killed young Matson?"

"Sanchez automatic, wasn't it? It's in the record."

"Sorry, Chief, it's not in the record. Are you sure about the Matson gun?"

"No, but I'm sure about the Melville gun. The Melville girl was killed with a Sanchez automatic. Nine millimeters. Five lands."

"All Sanchez automatics have five lands." James Lee tapped the desk impatiently with the bullet that had been fired at him the night before.

"What have you got?"

"This wire may leak. I can't tell you."

"Need any help?"

"Lots of it."

"I can have a dozen of your own men over from San Francisco in five hours."

"Too late. I need help but I've got to work alone. If anything happens to me cover the Sonora border south of Stanton. If you don't hear from me by eight o'clock tonight, our time, get busy."

"Okay. Standing by. Good luck."

James Lee hung up the receiver. He turned briskly to Al Blake.

"You heard that. Let's go!"

When the roaring car had warmed up on the first five miles of the return journey to Stanton, "What's that hunch of yours, Mr. Lee?" Al Blake asked again. "You think Flint is in Stanton?"

"I'm sure of it," James Lee said. "Flint and his gang pulled a couple of kidnappings last year—killed their victims each time. Young Matson was the first one. The Melville girl was the other—both killed with a shot from a Sanchez automatic."

"And that shot last night that was fired at you—a Sanchez pistol?"

Behind the wheel of the car, James Lee looked sideways for one second at Al Blake. "You're right," he said. "My hunch is that it was Dutch Flint who fired the shot last night, or someone using his gun.... Putting a few of the pieces together—if Flint was north of Redstone he'd have to come south to escape. The Department has the Utah country blocked. I figure he landed in Crystal and that Bancroft got a spot on him in that town. Flint probably learned that Bancroft was a government man. Flint broke into the cabin at Redstone and killed Bancroft. Bancroft probably came in while Flint was searching your desk for Bancroft's reports on him."

"And the next move?"

"Wait a minute. As soon as Flint killed Bancroft the town of Crystal got too hot for him. He moved out. He couldn't move north and there is nothing east or west.... He came south into Stanton—and his hideout is Bill Putnam's joint."

Silent thereafter for three minutes, "Mr. Lee, I've got a favor to ask of you," Al Blake said. "Just for luck, and because I thought a hell of a lot of Frank Bancroft, I'd like to sit in with you on this scrap."

James Lee reached around under his right armpit. With his left hand he hauled out a long blue-barreled .38. He handed the gun to Al Blake. "Here," he said, "take this—I've another one."

In Stanton at 6:15, directing the overture that preceded the first act of the big show, "I'm going to coast up within a hundred feet of Putnam's joint," James Lee began. "You cover the back end of the layout. I'm going in the front door. Don't let anyone get by you. Shoot first and challenge the corpse. I'll try to clean up in a hurry."

Ten feet inside the front door of the Pastime Club, James Lee made a quick survey of the long poolroom. Two players were at the first table. Half a dozen idle spectators sat in the armchairs that ranged along the wall.

The proprietor of the Pastime Club, Bill Putnam, was not present.

James Lee faced one of the loungers. "Mr. Putnam around?"

"He's in the back room."

At the door of the poker-room James Lee decided to enter without knocking. He twisted the knob of the door. The door was locked. A voice from within challenged him. "Who's there?"

"This is James Lee."

A moment later the door opened narrowly. "Come in, Mr. Lee. We've been waiting for you."

James Lee walked into the poker-room. Seated at a round table near the far wall of the room were two men. Putnam waved his hand at the first one, "You know Ben Carver, I believe.... Let me introduce Dutch Flint."

In spite of every effort James Lee heard his own indrawn breath hiss through his clenched teeth. Then calmly, "I'm glad to see you, Dutch," he said. "I've been wanting to meet you for a long time." He held out his hand to Dutch Flint.

"Keep your fins up in the air!" Dutch Flint ordered harshly. "Carver, frisk him!... Your foot sort of slipped this time, didn't it, Chink? You figgered I'd be hidin' under the bed in the back room! Sit down. I've always wanted to play table stakes with a G-man!"

James Lee looked at the scattered cards on the top of the poker table. "No," he protested, "everything is working out fine. I'll be glad to play a little poker before I turn in for the night."

"Sit down," Dutch Flint repeated. "Make yourself at home. When you turn in for the night you'll turn in for the big sleep."

"Don't be rude to your playmates, Dutch. When are you leaving town?"

"I'll be pulling out in a couple of hours."

"Fair enough. What are the chips worth?"

"Twenty bucks a stack."

"I'm a little short of cash at the moment," James Lee announced. "What's my gun worth?" He pointed to his long blue-barreled .38 that lay on the table at Dutch Flint's right hand.

"I'm banking," Putnam cut in. "I can't allow you anything on the gun. It belongs to Dutch—finders keepers, you know, wise guy."

"Fair enough. Give me a couple of stacks. Anything wild?"

"Nothing wild in this game but a G-man," Ben Carver answered. "We're all tame enough."

The lower rim of the conical green-glass lamp shade hanging twelve inches above the center of the table lay on a level with Dutch Flint's upper lip. James Lee saw Flint's mouth working under the stress of hate. "Dutch is getting wild," he said. "Maybe he's anxious about something. Deal the cards."

"You deal the cards, G-man. You win the deal."

James Lee reached for a new deck that lay at his left and broke the seals on it. "Not that I don't trust you gentlemen," he said, "but I like to train my own cards. I'm looking for aces.... Dutch, some place in your hand tonight you're going to find the seven of spades. You know what that card means."

"I ain't never lost yet, wise guy. It's your turn to lose tonight."

"Listen, Dutch—I can't lose! I can't lose and you can't win! The cards are stacked against you seven ways from the jack. Frank Bancroft is playing against you tonight. Young Matson is playing against you tonight. The little Melville girl is playing against you tonight. Every hand is stacked against you. You're yellow and you're rotten. You can't win!"

The fingers of Dutch Flint's right hand closed convulsively on the long blue-barreled .38 that lay on the table beside him. "Shut up, Chink!" he grated. "Shut up or I'll spill a slug of lead into your mouth!"

"Spill and be damned!" James Lee challenged.

Across the table Ben Carver looked at his watch. "How much longer is this going on?" he asked.

"What time have you got?" James Lee made the inquiry in a bland voice.

"Six-fifty, but time don't mean nothin' to you, does it?"

"It means a lot right now—I'm hungry. Anything to eat around here?"

Bill Putnam frowned. "Dutch, deal the cards!"

"I ain't so nuts about poker like I was. What about some chow? Me and the Chink is both hungry."

"There's no chow in the joint," Putnam announced. "Deal the cards. We got to do something for the next half hour or else we'll all go nuts."

Dutch Flint snarled. "Get up and get something to eat! I'm sick of waiting for that punk with the car."

Carver got up. "Wait a minute!" Dutch Flint halted him with a lifted hand. "When you get the sandwiches bring back a good long carving knife.... We don't want to use no guns on this Chink." Quickly to James Lee, "How about it, Chink? A knife under your ribs suit you just as good as a slug in the heart? Am I right?"

James Lee nodded. "Either way. It makes no difference to me—only I'm sorry to tell you, Dutch, if you let Carver go now he won't come back."

"What the hell do you mean?"

"What do you suppose I mean? I'm on the spot. I know the way out. I might as well tell you that there isn't a chance in a million that Carver will ever get back if he leaves this joint."

Half standing, Dutch Flint gave way to a moment's rage. He beat the poker table with both his fists. "Damn your yellow skin! Where do you get that stuff?"

"Take it easy. Sit down! Listen. Dutch, you don't suppose I came here without a mob, do you?"

Once more Dutch Flint reached for the blue .38. "Mob?" he snarled. "What mob?"

"Something less than a million men fore and aft. You don't think that you and I are the only strangers in town tonight, do you? If you've got guts enough to get out of this room, go have a look. Size up the street. Size up the vacant lot back of this joint."

Dutch Flint, with a puzzled frown on his face, turned to Bill Putnam.

"What do you think about this?" he asked. "What if he ain't lying?"

Putnam looked at the backs of five cards that lay on the table in front of him. Then he looked up at Ben Carver. "Go out and look around," he said. "We can't take no chances. Size up the street and then prowl around behind this joint. I'll let you in the back door."

To himself, "If I can get rid of one of them I've got a chance," James Lee decided.... "I wonder if Al Blake is on the job?... I've got to take a chance." To Carver, "Good luck! If you've got any last words for your surviving relatives, you'd better tell somebody about it."

Dutch Flint scowled. His glance ranged between Putnam and James Lee. "Can't you make him shut up? If you don't I will!" he said to Putnam.

Carver slid through the door and closed it. Bill Putnam got up and shoved the bolt that barred it.

There was a moment of silence. Then, striving with all his intellect to visualize Ben Carver's course and to calculate Al Blake's probable move in the next play, in a voice as steady and as cold as an arctic mountain, "Deal the cards, Dutch," James Lee invited. "I'll play you three hands—life or death."

Dutch Flint sneered. "You lose. You don't need no cards. You lose without any.... What time is it, Bill?"

Putnam looked at his watch. "Seven-twenty."

"That punk ought to be out in front with the car in ten minutes."

"Right. Listen, Dutch, you let me get out of here before you finish this Chink. I don't want to stretch for this, and besides that ..."

Interrupting, "You turning yellow? One more gob of gab like that and I spot you with the Chink. I've shot my way out of a mob of better men than you. Sit down!"

Is Al Blake on the job?

"Take it easy, Dutch," Putnam advised. "I was only trying to play safe."

"You're safe enough. Nobody's going to hurt you. You can get out of this job on half as good an alibi as the one you used when you croaked that Reno..."

Interrupting the Reno reminiscence, from the darkness of the vacant lot behind the Pastime Club, there sounded the heavy report of a black powder revolver cartridge. The sharper crack of a high-power shell exploding in Al Blake's weapon echoed the first shot.

On the instant that the first shot registered in his consciousness James Lee ducked under the poker table. He heaved against the lower rim of the table with his shoulder. As it went over against Dutch Flint he dived to catch the tumbling gun that had lain at Flint's right hand. He poked the gun upward and fired twice under Dutch Flint's left elbow. As his crumpling victim slumped down on him he swung the long, blue barrel of the heavy .38 dead to a line on Putnam's chest.

He wrestled his way out from under the body of Dutch Flint and got to his feet in time to answer a thunderous summons on the bolted door of the poker-room. He heard Al Blake's voice. "Open up! How about it, Mr. Lee? You safe?"

"Safe as a church," James Lee answered. He slid the bolt on the door and opened it. "How about yourself?"

"Carver burned me through the arm."

"Where is he?"

"I spiked him. He can stand a life sentence if they patch him up a little.... That's a great gun, Mr. Lee.... Who are these citizens on the floor?... Ah, one of them's Putnam, I see."

"That's the name. And the other is Dutch Flint," James Lee said slowly. "He's dead, too.... Go telephone for Sheriff Deane, will you, please? We can let him bungle the remaining formalities with confidence."

THE THIRTY THOUSAND DOLLAR BOMB

Staying over in the Palace Hotel in San Francisco for a week on his return from the Orient, Senator Colton of the Committee on Foreign Relations found time to indulge himself in a mysterious project for the good of the nation.

"Don't ask me any more questions and don't give me any more orders," he said in the manner of a petulant child, addressing his confidential secretary, Sylvia Deane. "The way you talk, anybody would think I was a freshman up to his neck in a vacation scrape. I know what I'm doing, darling. Lay off me!"

Masking a warmer, a more tender sentiment with a frown that failed to mar the beauty of her face, "You knew what you were doing the last four times that your affairs went haywire," Sylvia said. "You'd better let me in on this. These mammoth projects of yours usually need the wrecking crew sooner or later. What's the layout? Tell Mamma."

"I'll tell Mamma when the time comes. Right now you take your orders from Papa. Go out and get me thirty thousand dollars in currency and bring it back here quick. I'll meet you in this room. There's a gentleman in the next room who does not care to be seen."

"Who is he?"

"That's my business. You'll know all about this when the proper time comes. Go out and get the money for me. I'm ten years older than you are and twice your weight and if there is any more argument I'll knock you cold and throw the quivering remains in the Bay. Twenty-six is young to die. Get the money! Get it in fifties. Hurry up!"

Returning after a twenty-minute expedition to the Crocker Bank, Sylvia Deane handed Senator Colton a package of currency the size of a thin brick. "Here you are," she said. "The seals aren't broken. It's all there—and that's more than I can say for you."

The senator grunted. "That's the best-looking hat you ever wore," he said, smiling down at his secretary. "Wait here for a little while and I'll take you out to lunch."

"What about that mob of prominent citizens and sterling patriots in the parlor?"

"Jim can handle them. Wait here for me."

Reappearing seven minutes later, the senator handed Sylvia Deane a manila folder. "You take care of this," he said. "It's too hot for me to carry. If anything happens to me deliver these documents to the Secretary of State in Washington. When I say take care of these papers that's just exactly what I mean. I don't want you to turn them loose for a minute. Wear 'em! There may be a world war wrapped up in that package."

"Have I your permission to look them over?"

"Of course. Look them over but keep the dope under your hat. Permission to look them over! That's a silly request. I never keep anything from you."

"Who got the thirty thousand dollars for this stuff?"

Young Senator Colton smiled. He stuck out his tongue at his secretary. "That's my business," he said. "You know everything—but what you don't know won't get you bumped off."

"You sound like a movie gangster."

"I am," the senator declared. "Wait till the shooting begins and you'll be proud of your gangster."

At luncheon the senator evolved a scheme whereby he might avoid the thronging politicians who infested his suite at the Palace. "I'm going down the peninsula to Burlingame this afternoon and have dinner with Desmond Cross tonight," he announced.

"Don't drink too much," Sylvia said.

"I'm not going down to drink with him. What do you think of honoring his newspapers with ammunition enough to start the next campaign for the party?"

An eager look in the senator's eyes gave Sylvia Deane the cue for her next question: "These mysterious documents that I'm wearing at the moment—is that your ammunition?"

"Part of it."

"I'd go slow right now if I were you," Sylvia advised. "You decided yesterday that it was a little early to open the battle."

"I hadn't seen those documents yesterday. Read them this afternoon. You'll see what I mean. I'll bring Desmond back with me tonight. I'd like to have you wait up for us, if you will."

"I'll be on the job," Sylvia said. "If you'll drink your coffee your driver can set me down at the hotel before you start for Burlingame. I'm anxious to see these high-priced documents. Something tells me you've invested thirty thousand dollars in a luxury."

"Wrong again," the senator smiled. "Wait till you read 'em. They're dynamite! When Desmond Cross explodes them in his newspapers there will be enemy scalps hanging in the treetops from here to New York." The senator drained his second cup of coffee. He set the cup down with a bang. "Darling, maybe you know everything but you've still got a lot to learn. Them thar papers is bad medicine for some mighty big Injuns. Just plain poison."

Sylvia smiled wearily. "A lot of people have lived through an overdose of poison," she suggested. "Don't forget that."

"I never forget anything, my sweet little wet blanket. Come on—I'll take you back to the hotel and roll on down to Burlingame. You'd better telephone Desmond that I'm coming. He might have a golf date."

In the seclusion of her room in the senator's suite at the Palace, Sylvia Deane telephoned Desmond Cross at Burlingame and then, eagerly, she began to investigate the contents of the manila folder. There were seven documents in the folder. One of them was a typewritten manuscript of ten pages. The other six were variously written with pen and ink, typewritten, or typewritten with revisions in three different scripts. Two documents were in French, two more of them in German with revisions in what Sylvia judged to be Russian. The ten-page typewritten manuscript and the two remaining documents were written in English. She began reading the ten-page manuscript. When she had come to the bottom of the second page she glanced rapidly through the remaining portion with increasing haste. To the last page of the document whereon appeared three signatures she devoted a brief thirty seconds.

She reached for the telephone on her desk and called long distance.

"Burn a line through for me to Washington," she directed, and then, becoming explicit, "this is an official rush call for Bradford Garnett at the State Department. Senator Colton calling."

Enjoying precedence over other traffic, the call went through to Bradford Garnett in fifty-eight seconds. Instantly when she heard Garnett's voice, "Who is your hot spot ace out here?" Sylvia asked. "Is Seventeen still working in San Francisco?"

"Seventeen is on the other side of the Pacific," Bradford Garnett informed her. "What sort of a job is it? We have three men in San Francisco right this minute."

"The senator has bought some dynamite. Documents. Who is the high man in that game?"

"Chinese, six feet tall, weight one hundred and sixty-five pounds, Yale—name James Lee. His telephone number is China 7707. Ask for Lee Wong and say that Gettysburg is calling. Incidentally, how are you?"

"Thank you, Brad. I'm fine."

"Married or single?"

"Still single. Goodbye."

"Congratulations. Goodbye."

Thirty seconds after she hung up on the Washington call Sylvia rang through to China 7707.

Waiting, she fumbled mentally with the word Shenandoah but instantly when the call was answered, "I wish to speak with Lee Wong," she said. "Tell him Gettysburg is calling."

Then in even tones a vibrant voice over the wire said, "James Lee speaking," and suddenly Sylvia seemed to realize that the burden of her problem had shifted to stronger shoulders.

"This is Sylvia Deane speaking for Senator Colton. The senator has picked up some dangerous documents. When can I see you? Where can I see you?"

"Turn to your left from Grant Avenue at Jackson Street. A man will be waiting for you at the entrance of Ross Alley. He will guide you to my apartment."

At the door of James Lee's apartment, which was on the second floor of a building that stood on the west side of Ross Alley, Sylvia's guide knocked softly.

When the door opened, Sylvia faced a Chinese man who smiled at her. "I am James Lee, Miss Deane," he said. "Mr. Garnett called me from Washington since you telephoned me. I am at your service. What is your problem?"

The girl handed the manila folder to James Lee. "Senator Colton paid thirty thousand dollars for these documents. He is spending the afternoon with Desmond Cross. Do you know Desmond Cross?"

"I know him," James Lee said.

"Mr. Cross is coming back to San Francisco tonight with the senator to see these documents. Look at them. The senator intends to turn them over to Mr. Cross. Read them. You will understand what it might mean if the senator permits Mr. Cross to publish them in his newspapers. Read that ten-page affair first."

Halfway through the ten-page manuscript James Lee quit reading. He turned to the last page of this document and inspected the three appended signatures. "This is very interesting, Miss Deane," he said. "If it is authentic it means that Germany and Russia are better friends than Washington thinks."

Sylvia Deane frowned. "And what else does it mean?"

James Lee looked straight at the girl for a moment and then, "Probably another world war," he said quietly. After a moment, "If I remember correctly, the senator is inclined to specialize in luxuries of this kind."

"Do you refer to the Bernal papers?"

"I had forgotten that case. I was thinking of the French indemnity memorandum that upset the Geneva tea party."

Sylvia Deane nodded.

"They cost him a hundred thousand," she said. "I was too late to save him—that time."

"But this time—you flatter me."

"You will do what you can? It isn't the money—it's the..." Smiling then at James Lee, "It isn't the first cost of these things. It's the upkeep of the senator's self-respect among other things. I think he's been hooked. Won't you please see what you can do?"

"Where did he get them?"

"They were turned over to him this morning in one of his rooms at the Palace. I don't know who brought them to him. He paid thirty thousand dollars for them."

The tall Chinese closed his eyes for a moment.

"That has a reminiscent flavor," he said. "Let's go into my library and we'll have a better look at these little gems of literature."

Following James Lee into the room that he called his library, Sylvia observed that it was lighted by three windows in the west wall. Under these windows there was a long table littered with a miscellany of apparatus. The tall Chinese waved his hand toward the long table. "Cameras, microscopes, bottles, test tubes, junk in general—that's my stuff. All very portable when it's packed. First, let's have a look at this ten-page affair. I'll take a couple of photographs of the signature page and then I'll run a test on the paper. Nice clear typewriting, isn't it?"

"It's perfect work," Sylvia agreed. "Almost too perfect."

"That fact alone is significant," the Chinese declared. "Five or six of the big-shot forgery crew have tendencies toward perfection.... How much time have I on this job?"

"If the senator has dinner with Desmond Cross in Burlingame he won't be back until ten o'clock. They might decide to come back to the hotel for dinner. Five o'clock is the deadline."

"That gives me three hours. I can't read Russian script, can you?"

"Not a word of it."

When the signature sheet of the ten-page manuscript had been photographed, "That final paragraph alone is war material enough to start another scrap," James Lee said. "Specific aren't they! Listen: 'The Munitions Corporation of America guarantees to the governments of Russia and of Germany that high authority in government of the United States of America possesses full knowledge of the terms of this agreement and that the United States of America will in no way interfere with the deliveries of naval guns, salt, cotton or quicksilver to the ports designated.'"

James Lee scowled. "That's a big order," he declared. "I wonder who the high authority in government may be."

"That's probably the phrase that the senator paid for. You remember the documents that the senator procured covering the bribery of the Bolshevists by Germany."

James Lee nodded. "Quite well. Document Sixty-eight was the important one."

"You have a good memory," Sylvia complimented.

"I played a small part in that show," James Lee said.

"What do you make of this layout?" The Chinese waved his hand in the general direction of the six documents that lay to his left on the work table beside the manila folder. "Tell me in ten words. I have use for your opinion."

"It means that the United States rides with Germany and Russia against France and Japan."

James Lee nodded. "You ran over ten words but I agree with you. And what about England?"

"England may be fortunate enough to keep out of it—for a while. Then she would smash Japan—and France...."

"How about shoving all of these papers into the fire and telling Senator Colton that you lost them?" James Lee suggested.

Sylvia's eyes widened. "That's absurd," she said. "That wouldn't change anything. If these documents are forgeries they mean nothing. If they're authentic, destroying them would mean less than nothing."

James Lee smiled. "I will telephone to you at five o'clock," he said. "You had better return to the hotel now. If the senator is dining in Burlingame it will afford me more time to work on them. One way or another we shall have to prevent their publication." Then, observing a quick look of doubt in Sylvia's eyes, "Have no fear," he said. "I will return the documents to you. I think I can persuade the senator not to publish them."

"I cannot leave without them. I pledged my word to the senator."

"Right! I'll see what I can do with photographic copies and samples of the paper. You don't mind if I clip a sliver of paper from each one of them, do you?"

"Of course not. I'm sorry that I cannot let you keep the originals."

When James Lee had finished with his photography and after he had clipped sample slivers from the corners of each page of the documents Sylvia gathered up the seven documents and put them back into the manila folder.

At five o'clock, answering James Lee's inquiry, "The senator is on his way up here now with Desmond Cross," she said. "What luck?"

"So far not much luck," James Lee answered. "I'll call you later."

After he hung up the telephone he returned to the work table against the west wall of the room. He picked up the sliver of paper that he had clipped from the signature sheet of the ten-page document and dropped it into a small beaker. He poured an ounce of a dilute solution and boiled it for ten minutes. He poured off this liquid and washed the sliver of paper a dozen times in distilled water. He transferred the sliver of paper then to a small porcelain mortar and broke it up into a mass of fibers. He dried these between two sheets of filter paper. Then with a microscope needle he lifted a minute mass of these fibers to a glass slide. He stained the fibers with a zinc-chlor-iodine solution and put the slide on the stage of a microscope. He swung a one-eighth-inch objective into place and after a quick adjustment of the sub-stage mirror he focussed the instrument.

"Three blue fibers! Esparto grass in linen! That's funny. I wonder why that great patriotic organization known as the Munitions Corporation of America, operating in the grand old state of Pennsylvania, uses an English paper for its documents! Item one."

He wrote a brief note in a memorandum book. "Now," he said, speaking half aloud, "we'll have a look-see at the type faces that wrote this perfect manuscript."

Eight minutes after he began the study of this element of his work he placed a New York call and got his number after a four-minute delay.

"James Lee speaking," he said. "Locate some of the Garwood typewriter officials and find out when they shipped their first electric carriage machines to Germany. Find out the date those new models went on the market in the United States. Find out when the first delivery of these machines was made to the Munitions Corporation. That's all. Burn it through to San

Francisco—China 7707—wait a minute! Tell me what big shots in the forgery game are enjoying the climate of North America right now.... Wendell, 'London Red' Riley, Ceriga, Kameneff.... Wasn't Ceriga the man who specified currency in fifties in the Field blackmail case?... What—in San Francisco!..."

James Lee hung up the telephone and walked rapidly to the door of the room. In the hallway he turned to the left. At the far end of the hallway he opened the door of a room. In the room at the moment there were four men busily engaged in the great American game of trying to make two pair beat three of a kind.

"Hold the deal," James Lee ordered, smiling. "All bets are off for an hour or so. I want you to find Alexander Patros for me. Bring him in, if you find him. Five feet two, black hair, Greek, scar on the left of his chin, cigars, always tan shoes.... What else? Edwards, you know him better than I do."

"That's complete, Mr. Lee, except the trotting-horse watch chain—and Patros is an alias. Ceriga is his right name," Edwards answered.

"Check. You cover Third and Townsend. Mr. Walker, have a look at the airports. Mr. MacDonald, you and Mr. Stanley will get a line en the steamships. Where is young Mr. Francis?"

"He's probably at that joint on Grant Avenue."

"Drop in and tell him to go over to the Hall of Justice. Tell him to ask the police department on my authority to get a teletype order up and down the coast for Ceriga's arrest. No radio. The radio is out! You lose more fish than you catch with radio. Bring Ceriga, alias Patros, in here to me. That's all."

James Lee left the room and returned to his work table in the library of his borrowed apartment.

When Desmond Cross had finished reading the ten-page typewritten document, "This is the biggest piece of news that's busted since the Lusitania was torpedoed!" he exclaimed, facing Senator Colton and Sylvia Deane in the parlor of the senator's suite. "We've got to break it to the world tonight!"

The senator nodded. "Okay," he said. "Shoot the works."

To Sylvia Deane, "Please call Brook 6000, and tell Mr. Forest to come over here at once," Desmond Cross directed.

"He's the managing editor of my San Francisco paper. Tell him to send some photographers over here."

To the senator, "Forest will handle everything," he said. "The story will be on the streets of the world in the next hour."

Sylvia reached for the telephone and when Central had answered, "I want China 7707," she said, lowering her voice in an attempt to keep Desmond Cross from hearing the number that she called.

On the instant, alert, "That's the wrong number!" Cross exclaimed. "Call Brook 6000. Let me have the phone!"

Frowning at Sylvia, "What's the matter with you?" Senator Colton asked in a quick flash of anger. "You've been trying to gum up this deal for the last fifteen minutes. Explain yourself."

The girl's eyes seemed to darken for an instant. Then meeting the senator's glare with a flaming glance, "You'd better hold this deal, as you call it. Do you realize the risk you run? Both of you?" Directly to the senator, "If there's anything wrong with these documents you will be the world's champion fool. You'll be the big joke of two continents—until somebody's hired man blasts you full of lead!"

"Call Desmond's editor or give him the telephone!" the senator commanded.

"I'll sock him with the telephone! Take five minutes out of this battle, both of you, and use a little common sense. Use some of mine if you haven't any of your own! In the first place, no newspaper has a right to these documents. In the second place, if they're forgeries Mr. Cross will sell his papers easily enough, but there will be a broken-down ex-United States senator among the newsboys. What's your big target—another world war or a new administration? Both of you make me sick!" The girl jerked the telephone out toward Desmond Cross. "Here's your telephone. If you're fool enough to call your editor, call him!"

Cross took the telephone from Sylvia's hands. Hesitating, he turned to Senator Colton. "Are you sure these things are authentic?"

"Of course they're authentic!" the senator barked, but his voice seemed to lack its former element of dominant confidence. "Get your man up here."

Desmond Cross, enjoying a brief self-comforting moment of defiance, nodded at Sylvia Deane. When the operator answered him, "Brook 6000," he said harshly in the approved masculine manner. To his managing editor, "Rig the shop for a big story," he directed. "Please come up to Senator Colton's suite in the Palace at once. Bring some photographers with you. We want to plaster the front page with pictures of some documents."

Hanging up the telephone, he turned to Sylvia Deane. "Everything is all right, my dear," Desmond Cross began, pitching his voice to the tone he might use in soothing a child who had been robbed of a stick of candy.

A knock on the door of the senator's parlor interrupted him.

Sylvia opened the door to confront James Lee.

"We'll receive no one for the next hour," the senator ordered.

Ignoring this, "Come in, Mr. Lee," Sylvia invited; and when the visitor entered, "Senator Colton, let me introduce Mr. James Lee. Mr. Cross, Mr. Lee. Mr. Lee is on the coast for the State Department."

Bowing to Desmond Cross and to the senator, proceeding directly with his business, "Senator, the documents that Miss Deane submitted for my inspection are forgeries," the Chinese man announced.

In a new outburst of anger, "What the hell is all of this?" the senator exploded. To Sylvia Deane, "What have you done—sold me out? How did this Chinese happen to get a look at this stuff?"

In an even voice, "I showed them to him," Sylvia said.

Intervening before the senator could speak, "They are forgeries, Senator."

"What do you know about it?"

James Lee raised his eyebrows. "I beg your pardon," he said. After a moment's silence, "The documents are forgeries," he resumed.

"You're crazy," the senator contradicted. "How do you know they're forgeries? What right have you to..."

Interrupting the senator, James Lee raised his hand, and when the senator, impelled to silence, had cooled to a degree where he could comprehend plain language, "For one thing," James Lee began, "the ten-page manuscript was written on a typewriter that was not manufactured until eight months after the date of the document. I refer to the Munitions Corporation contract. The Garwood typewriter people began work on the type face used in the text of that document more than five months after the date of the document."

The senator frowned. "And what else?" he asked in a voice that had lost the resonance of rage.

"Several things," James Lee suggested. "The paper on which the document was written was manufactured in England. The Munitions Corporation stationery happens to be manufactured in a paper mill in Massachusetts." Then, abandoning his easy manner, "One moment, Senator—perhaps I have some additional evidence that may convince you."

The Chinese walked rapidly to the door of the room. He opened the door. Speaking quietly to a man in the hallway, "Mr. Walker," the Chinese said, "ask Mr. Edwards and Mr. Stanley to bring Ceriga up here," he directed.

Returning to face the senator, "A couple of my assistants picked up the man who sold you these documents. They found him at the Third and Townsend station. He was leaving for Los Angeles."

When Malio Ceriga, alias Alexander Patros, was brought into the room, handcuffed, to face the senator, "Tell your story, Ceriga," James Lee ordered. "Make it brief."

"The documents I sold you are forgeries," the Greek faltered. "I made them myself. I will give you back the money if you will use your influence to..."

"Enough of that!" James Lee interrupted sharply. Then to Senator Colton, "He has signed a full confession."

Nodding to his three men, "You can take him out," James Lee said. He reached into an inner pocket of his coat and hauled out a thick package of banknotes. "Here is your thirty thousand dollars." He handed the currency to Senator Colton. "You can reach Ceriga whenever you want for the next ten or fifteen years. He'll be in Alcatraz. He'll have to serve that long on another charge we have against him.".

James Lee turned from the senator and held out his hand to Sylvia Deane. "I'll bid you good night, Miss Deane," he said. "It's been a pleasure to have been of service—to you."

He nodded curtly in the general direction of Senator Colton. "Good night, sir," he said. "I hope you'll forgive Miss Deane for letting me in on this game."

"Just a second," the senator said. He got to his feet and held out his hand to James Lee. "Mr. Lee," he said, "west of the Rocky Mountains there is a strange animal known as a jasper louse. I apologize for being a jasper louse. I can't tell you how much I appreciate what you have done for me."

A moment after James Lee left, the senator pulled himself together with a visible effort. He walked toward a decanter of whisky that sat on a table against the west wall. He poured himself half a tumbler of bourbon, and then nodding at Desmond Cross, "You'd better join me," he said weakly.

When his companion had poured his drink, the senator lifted his glass toward Sylvia Deane. "I won't presume to drink this one to you, Sylvia," he said. "I'm using it for medicinal purposes only."

The girl smiled in the manner of a mother forgiving a wayward child. "Drink hearty," she said cheerfully.

The senator drank heartily, and then, with a bravado born of humility, facing Sylvia, "You see what you've gone and done!" he said. "You spoiled a big story for poor old Desmond!" Following up this new indictment, when he had set his glass down the senator reached into his pocket and hauled out the thick bundle of currency. With a threatening gesture he waved the bank notes toward the girl. "Thirty thousand dollars! You know what I'm going to do with this? I'm going to take it down to Shreve's and trade it for a diamond ring as big as your ear! Then I'm going to make you a present of the ring."

Sylvia shook her head. "Not in a million years," she said.

"I never accept presents from the members of the Committee on Foreign Relations."

The senator batted his eyes a couple of times. "Have it your way," he said. "If you don't want the ring as a present you'll have to take it as an engagement ring. Make up your mind and be quick about it! I'm tired of all this monkey business."

Hesitating a moment, Sylvia smiled at the senator. "If you're sure it will be a genuine diamond..." she began.

MEDIUM WELL DONE

An hour before dinner Helen King walked into Wong Sung's kitchen.

"No dinner tonight," she said. "I'm dining out."

"You papa not come home?"

"He's delayed two days."

"More better you bring eprybody here for dinner. Large turkey."

"I'm dining out. Everybody will be here for cocktails."

Wong Sung blinked his eyes at the thought of the wasted turkey. "Who am I to question the will of Heaven?" To Helen King, "You papa all right?" he asked.

"He seemed to be. Bring a lot of ice and everything for some old-fashioned cocktails. Mr. Blake likes that bourbon out of the old barrel."

"I fix eprything."

Walter Blake, the first guest to arrive, devoted sixty seconds to telling Helen King how beautiful she was and then, taking his cue from her mildly disinterested expression, he finished his greeting with a second one-way kiss that seemed to lack terminal facilities. All right. Such was the life of an arctic explorer. Something on her mind.

"Where does it seem to pain you the most—and what is it?"

"Sorry, darling." Helen King smiled warmly at Walter Blake and the arctic chill melted to an equatorial temperature. "I'm disappointed. Dad telephoned from Houston that he wouldn't get to San Francisco until Thursday. He's flying to Los Angeles tonight."

"More oil wells?"

"I guess so. He said something about another million-dollar Christmas present for me."

"It's tough to be rich! How about mixing one before the rest of the mob arrives?"

"Hop to it. I can use an old-fashioned to beat the band. Maybe two or three of them! Darling—I wish you'd run the show tonight. I want to dance. Do you want to telephone Sam out at Tait's that we'll be there?"

"We'll be there with bells on! Tait's has a new name, you know—they call it the Edgewater Beach Club."

"It will always be Tait's to me—until they change the moonlight and the surf—and Sam."

Here was a cryptic signal, understood by two young people. It resulted in a clinch. Coming out of it, "There never was a night like that," Walter Blake said wistfully. "Why can't we be married right away?"

"Please mix the cocktails. Wipe the rouge off your lips. You look silly.... There goes the bell. Mix a string of them. We have some more customers."

Helen King's guests gave the demon rum a brief run for his money, and then, pleased with the idea of dancing through dinner, eight of the party voted yes on the Edgewater Beach Club proposal.

"There will be ten in our party," Walter Blake said, telephoning the club to confirm his reservation.

By eleven o'clock Helen King's guests had satisfied their appetites for food and drink and had danced until, in spite of the excellent orchestra, half of them elected to seek some greener field of pleasure.

Helen King nodded a quick acquiescence to a suggestion that the party seek a new port of call. She turned to Walter Blake in time to interrupt a burst of economics that he was orating into the cute ears of Jane Westlake.

"The quickest way to discover what will happen in Washington is to consult a fortune teller. Nobody knows exactly what..."

From across the table a green-eyed brunette charted the course for the next leg of the voyage.

"That idea hooks me! There's a woman down on the Marina that everybody is perfectly mad about. She's a Russian. She isn't a fortune teller, exactly, but she has the queerest place. Charlie Bent told me about her."

"What's her name?"

"Her name is Rousseau—Olga Rousseau. She's in the phone book. I'll tell her we'll all be down. She won't even ask who's in the party but I'll bet she'll know our names!"

The eyes of the blond girl seated beside Walter Blake widened with delight. “How do you suppose she does it?”

“Let's find out,” Blake suggested. Turning to Helen King, “Shall we take a whirl at this mysterious Rousseau bet, darling?”

“Of course! Everybody seems to like the idea. Let's go!”

Within three minutes after the green-eyed brunette had telephoned Olga Rousseau, a feminine voice rang through to the Edgewater Beach Club.

“What guests are included in that party of ten just leaving? I want the information for the society page of the Chronicle.”

When the information had been given Olga Rousseau hung up her telephone and devoted the next eight minutes to research relative to Helen King.

“Concentrate on her, Lily; the rest of them aren't important,” she said to a Negro woman. “I know enough about three of them to take care of everything. This looks like easy money.”

Lily, the Negro woman, smiled. “Catch 'em young,” she agreed, diving into the personal data section of Olga Rousseau's elaborate reference library. “Where will you receive them?”

“In the small parlor. Turn on about four lights—the pink ones. Rig Little Starlight for the preliminary and bring her in with a dash of thin violin and a spot of baby voice here and there.”

Without looking up from the pages of a book from whose text she was recording brief extracts in clean and beautiful shorthand.

“Thank God for that radio rig,” Lily said. “It never gets sore throat right when you need a baby voice.”

“Go easy with it,” Olga Rousseau admonished. “Let the kid chirp three or four times and then I'll rig the play as I go along. Don't go too heavy on the dramatics when you wake me up. These people are foxy eggs.... This Marshall King money is the biggest bet we've played since the Detroit cleanup.”

Leaving his disappointed turkey cooling under a dish towel, Wong Sung rode the Washington Street cable car down toward Chinatown an hour after Helen King had left her house. In the Grant Avenue colony of his countrymen, Wong Sung invested in a ten-cent lottery ticket for the nine o'clock drawing. Thereafter, until the gods of Luck might smile upon his investment with benevolent humor, or frown upon it, Wong Sung regaled himself with two cups of potent black brandy. He drank the first one for therapeutic purposes. He lifted the second cup of liquor in a ceremonial gesture aimed at complimenting a Chinese visitor, who at the moment was a guest of the Cave of Harmony. This club, whose membership included fifty members of the Wong family, counted this visitor, James Lee Wong, as its most distinguished cousin.

To his countrymen James Lee Wong was a member of the Wong family justly entitled to all the social advantages of the name, but to the public at large and on the federal pay rolls, the guest in the Cave of Harmony was more simply James Lee. Just now it appeared that Mr. Lee was interested in discovering the agency through which an important shipment of opium had been landed in San Francisco.

Mr. Lee spoke freely and without reserve. His companions were equally voluble in discussing the problem, so that within the hour three leads had been developed that promised to uncover enough evidence to convict a principal and two of his assistants in the affair.

From this interesting assemblage, at five minutes after nine, Wong Sung withdrew to have a look at the luck that his lottery ticket had brought. He discovered that his ten-cent investment was a total loss. “Fortunes are built on diligent labor,” he reflected. “Hola! The eyes of the blind need no ointment.” He returned forthwith to his master's house to enjoy the gift of sleep.

Speaking to Helen King and her companions through the lips of Olga Rousseau, Little Starlight lingered for a while on the topography and the flora of the spiritual world. Following this she related more specifically the details of her recent meeting with Mark Twain and Benjamin Franklin. The climate of the spirit plane, comparable in some respects to that of California, engaged her for a moment and then, remarkably technical for an Indian maiden, she favored her earth friends with the architectural details of a white marble structure whose iridescent floor glowed with the soft colors of a precious pearl:

"The marble temple is half hidden with rose vines. Spirits walk through its corridors. In the center of the great hall there is something draped with laurel and great wreaths, wreaths of red flowers. I do not know—Yes! It is the spirit world ceremony for an earth visitor!

"The red flowers cover the earthling's casket. There is beautiful music. The earth man is awaking. I see him. He is tall and slim. He has a lovely face. Gray hair. He is quiet and dignified and now he rises from his casket. He seems to recognize a lot of spirits who were friends of his on earth. They greet him joyously. They are taking him on a tour of the spirit world. The music is growing fainter.... I cannot hear it now. It is getting cold. I am going to..."

Interrupting Little Starlight, "What is the earth man's name who just arrived in the spirit world?" Walter Blake asked.

"I heard them speak his name," Starlight answered. "I cannot tell you. It would bring you pain and give you fear. Goodbye, beloved friends of earth. I will speak with you again. Little Starlight loves you."

With the definite object of shaking Helen King out of her wide-eyed mood, "Adios, Little Starlight," Walter Blake said abruptly. "So long, kid. We'll be seeing you."

At this, struggling out of the seeming trance that had rendered her rigid, Olga Rousseau fell sideways from her chair. Blake picked her up. The woman, heavy in his arms, looked up at him in bewilderment.

"Someone frightened Little Starlight," she said tearfully. "Oh, I am so tired!"

"Who is Little Starlight?" Blake asked.

"Please do not bother me with questions! I am utterly exhausted." From the couch on which Blake had laid her, Olga Rousseau smiled toward her guests. "I am sorry," she whispered.

"We'll be running along now. Thank you ever so much. A most interesting experience," Blake said.

Halting a moment beside her hostess, "I think you were perfectly wonderful," Helen King added. "The children's voices were so sweet!"

Olga Rousseau smiled at Helen King. "I'll see you soon again, my dear," she said.

At Van Ness Avenue, two middle-aged, leather-lunged newsboys were bellowing an extra. Walter Blake stopped his car and bought a copy of the Chronicle. Across the top of the paper, "PLANE CRASH KILLS THREE," he read. "California Oil Man, Pilot, Secretary, Die in Take-Off at Houston Field." Blake flashed one look at the leading paragraph that followed and then to Helen King, "The Arabs are at it again," he lied. "That was a wasted nickel." He stuffed the newspaper into his coat pocket and drove Helen King to her residence.

When the girl was safe in the living room of her house, Blake excused himself on the pretext of digging up a highball. He went to the telephone in Wong Sung's kitchen and put through a call to the Houston airport. When he had verified the newspaper report of the accident he called the physician who had attended Helen King through her various minor illnesses.

"This is Walter Blake speaking. I am calling from Marshall King's residence. Mr. King was killed in an airplane crash two hours ago. I haven't told Helen about it yet.... Will you telephone for a nurse?... Yes, I'll break the news to her now."

Eleven days after Marshall King's funeral, Helen King called alone at Olga Rousseau's house. She left the place within the hour and her eyes which had been dull with sorrow were shining now with the false light of some new hope that she had derived from her conference with Olga Rousseau.

Before Helen King had reached her own home after this visit, Olga Rousseau put through a call to Chicago for the proprietor of the Sterling Gold Finance Company.

"You tell The Kick to start for 'Frisco right away," she said. "The Kick—not the Kid. Kick Konrad, you big tin ear.... What do I care if he's at work on a job! Tell him I said to drop it and head west! That's all, Andy. Goodbye!"

Olga Rousseau hung up the telephone and turned to Lily who stood beside her. "Konrad always was a fool," she commented. "From what Andy said he's messing around with another kidnapping job. That bird will get his neck stretched yet."

"He never had any brains of his own," Lily agreed. "When do you expect him?"

"Four days from now or I'll see that he burns."

"What are you going to do when he gets here?"

"Plenty! Your job right now is to get a line on Marshall King's voice. Your best lead is to mix up with the Pullman boys. He used to ride The Lark from here to Los Angeles a lot."

"I've got his voice. It had a Middle-Western whang to it that got husky after he had three or four drinks. Soft Tennessee 'r,' and always keyed low. He never talked loud in the pinches."

"A man worth fifty million dollars doesn't have to talk loud. Where did you get the dope?"

"I was out last night with a chauffeur that drove him for eight years. Incidentally, I picked up the song Mr. King used to sing when he was doing a little drinking, or a little thinking, or when he was just plain happy. It is unusual enough to be convincing."

"You get the music?"

"Listen, honey!" In a rich, low voice Lily sang:

"'He always did the best he could,
He always said that he would try;
And so this little caterpillar,
He became a butterfly.'

"That was one of them. His sentimental song was that Sweet Rest thing:

"'On the other side of Jordan,
In the green fields of Eden,
Where the Tree of Life is blooming,
There is sweet rest for me.'"

"That's good work. Post The Kick on the music. That Jordan thing has a pull to it."

"Are you going to work The Kick as soon as he comes, Miss Olga?"

"Not by a long shot! We'll save him for the big play. Lily, unless I'm a sap, we'll be ready to pull the blow-off after the beautiful Helen gets three or four more loads of Little Starlight stuff."

"But, darling," Walter Blake protested, "there is nothing supernatural about that Rousseau woman! Look at the thing calmly and rationally."

Staring at Blake, speaking in a voice without emotion, "I believe in her," Helen King said. Her eyes were soft with tears.

Blake realized the futility of argument.

"Maybe you'd be happier if Jane Westlake or Louise or some one of the older women lived here with you for a while. It's too big a house. You shouldn't live alone. Maybe you ought to travel for a year. Why won't you marry me now that you need me? I hate to think of you alone through all these hours and..."

"Good night, darling," Helen King interrupted. "I'm not... quite alone." Quickly then, speaking to mask her statement, "Wong Sung is here. He's been a dear, the poor old thing."

When Walter Blake had left the house, Wong Sung, the poor old thing, elected once more to intrude upon his sorrowing mistress.

"More better eprybody come here see you now," he suggested. "You likee I make large dinner, eprybody come?"

"Go to bed," Helen King answered, smiling forlornly at Wong Sung.

On this night, instead of obeying orders, Wong Sung waited for an hour and then, at eleven o'clock, he left the house for a quick visit to the Cave of Harmony on Grant Avenue. He was gratified at discovering James Lee present in the assembly.

"This is a fortunate moment for me," he said in his greeting to the younger man. "I desire to consult you relative to a matter that concerns the happiness of my mistress."

"You do me great honor," James Lee said, following the ritual of right conduct. "How may I be of service to you?"

Wong Sung led the younger man to an inner room apart from the garrulous assemblage in the Cave of Harmony.

"With commendable filial devotion my mistress still permits herself to be torn by the claws of the demons of despair. She is a crushed flower. In her anguish she has sought assistance for her tortured spirit from an unworthy source."

"What would you have me do?" James Lee asked.

"The man she loves seems powerless to help her," Wong Sung answered. "Unless I am mistaken, she has been drugged with the nectar of spurious hope. Her will is broken, her reason seems to sleep. Even as an opium eater returns forever to the origin of his own hell, so has my mistress surrendered to a charlatan who gives her momentary release from the realities of her sorrow."

"Who is this person from whom your mistress seeks the gift of peace? You say Miss King is to marry Walter Blake? Has Mr. Blake no knowledge of the affair? Has he done nothing?"

"What can he do? His methods and his weapons would conquer a tangible enemy. They are futile against a foe from the spirit world."

James Lee nodded in quick decision. "I will help you," he said. "I have engaged enemies from the spirit world before."

Wong Sung bowed to his companion. "I cannot express my gratitude."

Four days after Kick Konrad landed in San Francisco, Little Starlight, with characteristic Indian courtesy, guided Marshall King through the pearly labyrinths of the spirit plane; then down to earth to where, in the little parlor of Olga Rousseau's house, Helen King sat waiting to hear her father's voice.

"The earth mists are cold," Little Starlight protested. "It has been dark and chill since we left the radiant realm of the spirit plane. I am unhappy. I grieve in sympathy for the sorrowing spirit who is beside me. He was so recently an earthling that he has not yet forgotten all the cares he knew on the earth plane. I must return now to the radiant warmth of the spirit plane. I will leave my sorrowing companion. He will speak to you. Goodbye, beloved friends of earth. Little Starlight loves you."

In the little parlor of Olga Rousseau's house thereafter for fifty seconds there was a tense silence. The silence was broken then by a faint moaning and a patter of incoherent, whispered words from Olga Rousseau's lips. Presently, more clearly, "I am trying.... I am striving to do your will," Olga Rousseau whispered. "I cannot speak for you—speak to us. You are here. Speak to us. You are torturing me—speak to us."

Helen King sat forward in her chair. The nails of her clenched hands bit deeply into the pink flesh of her palms. Then a voice spoke to her, faintly at first. Then, seeming to strengthen with the vibrant emotion of love, "Helen, Helen, my dearest Helen. My beloved daughter—I am so happy to be with you again."

"Your father speaks to you," Olga Rousseau whispered.

"Oh, Father, come to me! I want to see you. Come near me. Let me touch your hand!"

"I will come to you presently, my dear. I cannot visit you on the earth plane until every transgression, every sin, every fault of mine, is forgiven. I will come to you some day and hold your hand. But before that day my earth life must be purified. One earth spirit still doubts me. He thinks I injured him long years ago and where there is doubt we of the spirit plane cannot appear."

"What keeps you from me, Father? What is it that troubles you?"

"The barrier between us is a debt that I owe to an earth-ling who befriended me—a debt of gratitude and of money."

"Who is the man?"

"He is John Kellogg. He had faith in me in a moment of disaster. He loaned me money. I repaid the loan but he has never shared the profits of the first venture that was the foundation of my fortune. You were a little girl and you knew nothing of the source of my wealth, but from the money that John Kellogg loaned me I made my first fortune. In equity and fairness half of the profits from that venture should have gone to him. Until that debt is paid I cannot come to you."

"Where is this man? What sum do you owe him? Speak to me! Father, if you knew how I long to touch your hand just for a moment once again, these trifles would not keep you from me!"

Abandoning generalities, the spirit of Marshall King spoke in the specific terms of a bank president. The debt of gratitude could not be well defined but John Kellogg's share of the profits from the money that he had loaned Marshall King amounted to three hundred thousand dollars. Mr. Kellogg could be reached in care of the Sterling Gold Finance Company of Chicago. Having set forth this data the spirit of Marshall King retreated from a sudden chill blast that seemed to descend upon his section of the Happy Hunting Ground.

For a moment thereafter communications from the unseen world were relayed through Little Starlight, whose robust physique rendered her immune to the rigors of the climate of the spirit land.

Little Starlight's voice faded out on a swelling melody from the vibrant strings of a muted violin. Then, pulling herself together with evident effort, Olga Rousseau blinked her eyes at Helen King and voiced a well-timed plea for help in a strained voice as she collapsed in a dead faint.

Set against a longer list of negative characteristics, the proprietor of the Sterling Gold Finance could rightfully lay claim to the virtues of punctuality and good judgment. Playing the game, he rang through from Chicago on long distance promptly at the appointed moment and spoke to Olga Rousseau.

"It came," he said. "A cashier's check for three hundred grand. What's the next move?"

"Hold out thirty grand for yourself and express the rest of it to me in currency."

"What's the next chapter?"

"You'll know when the time comes, Andy. Play your hand. Goodbye."

Olga Rousseau turned to face Lily and Kick Konrad. "So far, so good," she announced. "Little Starlight wins another bet. Andy has got the dough. He'll express the rebate in currency tonight."

Kick Konrad reached for a whisky bottle that sat on the table in front of him and poured himself a drink.

"That's swell work, Olga," he said. "Two hundred and seventy grand! In the bag without a struggle. Where are you two dames heading for after the pay-off?"

"We're not heading. Listen, you rat, this is pin money. If I can rope her into making a will we bump her off with a realistic suicide effect and the big play is good for a million apiece."

"As far as I'm concerned there won't be any big play. You know what happens to repeaters. When that coin gets here I blow!"

"You'll stick like a good dog or you'll burn!" Olga Rousseau delivered her ultimatum with a spice of emotion.

"Yes, indeed, you'll burn," Lily corroborated. "We'll tell you when school lets out. Git yourself rigged with a make-up for the big reunion scene. You'd rather be Marshall King in Heaven wouldn't you, than Kick Konrad in Hell?"

Kick took another drink. Then surrendering, "I'll ride," he said. "Where's them pictures of King? How do you want him to show? White robes?"

"White robes," Lily confirmed, "and be careful not to burn yourself with the phosphorus."

"We pull the big play in this dump?"

"Not by a mile and a half," Olga Rousseau said. "The next act in this gold-bearing drama will be played in the King residence. And listen, Kick—if your travels take you up to the boudoir see that you keep your hooks off the sucker's jewelry! The spirits don't wear diamonds much in Heaven."

Departing from his accustomed routine, late on Thursday afternoon, Wong Sung devoted nearly an hour to sharpening his pet meat cleaver. Earlier in the day, emerging from the Cave of Harmony after a consultation with James Lee, old Wong Sung invested sixty cents in the purchase of a fine-grained carborundum stone. Now, working diligently, he developed a razor edge along the ten-inch blade of his favorite cleaver. Presently he noted to his disgust that the thinned metal had become a wire edge. When this fault had been corrected he sheathed the narrow blade of the cleaver in a little teakwood trough lined with cork and set about the business of preparing dinner for his mistress.

With the coffee that Wong Sung served to Helen King, "You may go out tonight," the girl said. "I shall not need you. Nobody but Miss Rousseau is coming."

"You no likee me stay I go see my cousin. Mister Blake not come see you?"

"Not tonight," Helen King said. "He is busy in his office."

"What for he no come?" Old Wong frowned at this evident neglect on the part of Walter Blake. "More better he come see you epry night. More better you get married. Allee time too much stay all alone. Allee time cry like small child. I think you very happy get married."

Making appropriate allowance for the personal qualities of the old servant's advice, "Some day maybe I'll get married," Helen King said slowly. For a moment there was a wistful smile on her lips and then, more directly, "If Miss Rousseau is still here when you return you need not come in to see us. We shall want nothing."

At nine o'clock that night, twenty minutes after Olga Rousseau arrived, Helen King turned out all of the lights in the long living room. At Olga Rousseau's direction she locked the front door of the house and switched off all of the lights in the hallway except one.

"Sit here in this chair near me," Olga Rousseau directed. "Help me with your own will. It will be very difficult."

"I'll help you," Helen King answered. "Maybe Little Starlight will guide him to me."

Olga Rousseau did not answer, for her body had suddenly gone rigid. There was a moment of silence after this and then, from an unseen source, Helen King distinctly heard the low, soft music of a violin playing the air that seemed to be Little Starlight's favorite. She heard a child's voice singing and then, in deeper tones, she heard her father's voice singing the well remembered words of his favorite song:

"On the other side of Jordan,
In the green fields of Eden,

Where the Tree of Life is blooming,
There is sweet rest for me."

Impulsively, half rising from her chair, "Father, come to me!" Helen King whispered. "Come to me now!"

Marshall King's voice was low. "I am coming, my dear; I am happy now," he said. "The error that barred me from the earth plane is no longer in my pathway. I am coming to you, my beloved child. It is dark.... It is dark here on the earth plane. The spirit world is so light and beautiful. It is dark and cold here in this shadowed vale.... Reach out your hand, my daughter. Guide me to your arms."

Marshall King's voice seemed to come from the darkened doorway that opened into the entrance hall of the house. The tones of his voice increased in strength and then, trembling with the quick shock of surprise, through the wide eyes of fear, Helen King saw her father's figure entering the room. The returning spirit, clad in a luminous white robe, seemed to glide slowly toward. The girl saw that her father's face glowed with some faint unearthly light and that he seemed to smile at her.

"Here I am," she said, rising from her chair.

"I am coming to you, my darling. It is dark, so dark here on the earth plane. Stretch out your hand.... The darkness deepens. I must take you with me to the world of light when I return.... I cannot see you. This earth is as dark as a tomb of death."

Instantly, then, the dark room lightened. There was a click of an electric switch and Helen King saw the gliding apparition become violently animate. She heard a calm voice speaking:

"Stick 'em up, Konrad! Stay where you are, Rousseau."

James Lee stood in the open door of the dining room. In his right hand Helen King saw a long, blue-barreled thirty-eight. The weapon was leveled at Olga Rousseau. Walter Blake stood back of James Lee. Helen King called to Blake, and then she fainted. In her last moment of consciousness she observed the seven-foot leap made by her father's white-robed spirit.

In the entrance hall of the house there sounded a sudden chatter of guttural Chinese from the throat of old Wong Sung and an oath from Kick Konrad. The zipping impact of three blows of Wong Sung's cleaver followed. Hearing this James Lee, hardened as he was to violence, winced. He snapped a pair of handcuffs on Olga Rousseau's wrists. Leaving her under Walter Blake's guard, he walked into the hallway of the house. He saw old Wong Sung standing above a prostrate white-robed figure. The older Chinese raised his eyes and smiled at his countryman.

"I ketchum," he said to James Lee, and in his tone there sounded the mild pride of a modest victor.

James Lee stooped and laid his fingers on Kick Konrad's wrist. "You caught him plenty!" he said to old Wong Sung. "He's dead."

Accepting this manifestation of the will of Heaven, Wong Sung blinked his eyes.

"Large man die small fashion," he suggested. "Killum very easy."

In his report over long distance to his chief in the Department of Justice, "We got the Rousseau woman and Lily Lincoln, her Negro assistant," James Lee said. "We recovered all the money that had been taken from Miss King. Operative Miller arrested Andy Smallmann in Chicago. He was Rousseau's agent. Anton Konrad resisted arrest. It became necessary for my assistant in the case, Wong Sung, to use force in making the capture. Wong Sung is entitled to half of the reward for this criminal.... No. He hit him in the head with a meat cleaver."

That night in the Cave of Harmony there was a nine-course banquet. At the head of the banquet board, host to twenty of his admiring countrymen, Wong Sung related his version of the King-Rousseau case.

"Imagine my surprise to discover that the gods of Justice had placed a keen-edged weapon in my hand at the very moment that I needed something of the kind to sever the tentacles of the octopus that had fastened upon my mistress!"

"A wise man understands a nod," one of the guests suggested.

"Aye!" old Wong Sung agreed. "How great a blessing is clear perception!"

CPSIA information can be obtained
at www.ICGtesting.com
Printed in the USA
BVHW031139230121
598422BV00008B/1463